THE FREEDOM IN AMERICAN SONGS

THE
Freedom
in
AMERICAN
SONGS

STORIES

Kathleen Winter

A JOHN METCALF BOOK

BIBLIOASIS
WINDSOR, ONTARIO

FIRST EDITION

Library and Archives Canada Cataloguing in Publication

Winter, Kathleen, author
    The freedom in American songs : stories / Kathleen Winter. --
First edition.

Issued in print and electronic formats.
ISBN 978-1-927428-73-3 (pbk.).--ISBN 978-1-927428-74-0 (ebook)

    I. Title.

PS8595.I618F74 2014   C813'.54   C2014-902921-7
                                                C2014-902922-5

Edited by John Metcalf
Copy-edited by Allana Amlin
Typeset by Chris Andrechek
Cover designed by Kate Hargreaves

Biblioasis acknowledges the ongoing financial support of the Government of Canada through the Canada Council for the Arts, Canadian Heritage, the Canada Book Fund; and the Government of Ontario through the Ontario Arts Council.

PRINTED AND BOUND IN CANADA

MIX
Paper from
responsible sources
FSC® C107923

For my daughters

Contents

Part One
The Marianne Stories

A Plume of White Smoke

Frost on the kitchen window sparkled against the darkness. The Hallorans' porch light shone through crystal patterns. Marianne got up to put small junks in her stove. In her hands the birch sticks twined around each other like lovers' limbs. When she lifted the damper and threw the sticks in, they cried like live lobsters. How she loved her black stove with its deer and trees on its door.

This time last year, she'd lived between a manmade pond and Her Majesty's Penitentiary, in an apartment that reeked of methane—the window had looked out on a transformer tower and a procession of clouds like swans with dangling necks. If she didn't write something soon and sell it, she'd have to go back to town and work in some dismal office, and it would not matter at all whether any of the women in this harbour ate her berries or bread.

The time she took buns next door, Mrs. Halloran had run to the pantry with them, shoving her husband and stepson away like cats. She'd made no mention of the buns and Marianne wondered if she'd thrown them out. She'd once given Mary an apple pie and Mary sat looking out her window at the snowbirds eating rolled oats, not acknowledging Marianne's gift—lovely lattice pastry—except that she touched the pie now and then while commenting on the view: "What a critch that Vardy youngster has on him," or, "I love to watch the rocks come up through the melting snow ..." as if she were measuring phases of the moon.

The time Marianne brought Mary a jar of raspberries, Thomas sat slurping tea out of his saucer, the grizzles on his chin grey and shaggy like a January juniper.

"What's this?" he droned. He snuffled and opened the jar with fingers swollen and cut from mending nets. Raspberry juice dribbled onto the speckled Formica. The berries were scarce in January. "Hmph. Strawberries. No, raspberries. What'd you put them up in? Are they cooked?"

"No. Sugar and water."

He dropped the lid and left the jar mute in its juice puddle. You had to "put them up" in sugar and water—at least she'd done that right—but then you were supposed to boil them until the mess turned dark and shiny. Tom had the stove shaking with heat. Marianne spied long johns, nightdresses and a grandchild's baby clothes hung on a banister to dry. The stovepipe glowed red like iron in a foundry; missing rivets revealed a white inferno.

Marianne's stove was not like that. She did have good, creamy splits for lighting it. One of the young fishermen, Ezekiel, came up with his axe and cleaved them for her. Ezekiel had taken her with his pony and sled into the woods to cut the birch and some dry softwood.

Her lover from town said the new wood was an improvement on the rotten wood that she'd found by herself on the forest floor and that had filled her house with smoke. He didn't know Ezekiel had taken her on his horse to cut it. The pony had waited patient on the path, winter sun suspended between his ears. Marianne hung her scarf on a fir bough. She hadn't a clue what to do with an axe. Ezekiel showed her where to stand.

"Put some swing in it," he said. Ezekiel swung twice and the tree slowly cracked, then rustled, falling. She watched him scoop a mound of snow and wash his mouth out with it. After this he referred to her as "the little beaver." Now, each time she held a piece of the birch, she felt the sun's power in her hand.

The day after he helped her bring in the wood, Ezekiel came over and started making splits. He cut slices even as bread, then divided each slice into creamy fingers, using the axe delicately.

"I never saw such beautiful splits." Tom's splits and Mrs. Halloran's, too, were rough and uneven.

Ezekiel grew embarrassed. "It's all according to what kind of wood you makes it out of."

"I thought everyone had the same kind of wood."

"You wouldn't make splits out of a junk that was full of knots." From the pile he took a smooth junk. "You want one like this." He touched a knotty piece with the axe, "Not that." He'd stacked all her wood neatly: she'd left it in the pile where it had tumbled from the sawhorse. Then he taught her to make shavings.

He'd seen her prepare to make the shavings with an ordinary knife, and had cried out, "Come on, boy, invest in a hunting knife for making your shavings. You can't do it with that." Then, when he saw her hold the stick and slide the knife toward herself, "Don't get a hunting knife then if you're going to use it like that!"

"Trust me to do a thing the queer way," she said. In the cove, people still used the word in its old sense.

"Will this do?" She took up her breadknife. With a rag wrapped around its handle it made decent shavings. She made them as he'd shown her, thumb under the handle and tucked under her fingers, and long, clean strokes away from her. The shavings curled long and white, and when you made seven or eight on both sides of a stick, then the split looked lovely, tendrils arching off it like a Japanese lantern.

Now she laid her splits in a springy pile on the carved kitchen chair. They were so beautiful, and she had extra ones now, she considered taking a load to old Mrs. Ruby in the morning. How she'd met Mrs. Ruby was that Mrs. Ruby had dashed out of her house—once the old shop and post office—a pair of scissors in one hand, yelling, "I need a bit of that dress for one of my mats. Come in for a cup of tea while I cut a strip off it." Her kitchen was full of bright rags and yarn, a hooked mat half-finished on its frame. When Marianne finished that first cup of tea, Mrs. Ruby pretended a ball-end of green yarn was a teabag, tossed it in Marianne's cup, made as if to pour the kettle over it and said, "Have another cup before you go."

Now Marianne looked out at the sky. Moon-edged clouds tilted and collided over the swaying trees—the whole outdoors slid and crashed and moved. She had to go out in it.

Trees and wind, the wind heavy and wet through the spaces with a swoosh: snow had melted, revealing corn-coloured grasses down by the church. She started the graveyard way but the grasses drew her. She knelt and stroked them. The moon reflected in melting ice-puddles among the straw, nearly full.

A pointed boulder loomed high near the house no one lived in. When a car passed, the apple tree's branches extended in shadow over the clapboard. Above, the great bear glittered in his slow career. Below and all around, the dark spruce hid in their thicknesses deep mysteries. The islands called to each other with omnipresent gonglike voices. She knew the something she was looking for was happening. It was this. It was this night. She took the roadway home, over the hilltop that was always deserted, under a reeling sky; fences undulating overhill and dark twin spruce in the downhill sea-meadow.

One of Mrs. Halloran's cats crouched on the pine plank under the lilac tree in Marianne's yard. It liked to sharpen its claws on the bark. Mrs. Halloran never turned her porch light out until all her cats were called home. Two sat inside now on a sill—Marianne watched them from her bedroom window, silhouetted between Mrs. Halloran's orange curtains and the glass. *Lucky cats*, Marianne thought. *Nobody expects you to say anything*. A cat could roam the harbour intoxicated by lilac trees, grasses, phosphorescent lights in the sea, and not have to explain itself or make sense to any neighbours. She undressed, slid into the cold bed, and turned over and over until she found the exact position in which she always fell asleep.

*

The morning came brisk, all mildness of the day before gone. She lit her fire for the first time with the new splits Ezekiel had cut for her, then put the shavings for Mrs. Ruby in a Foodland bag. They jutted out of the top so she slid another bag upside down over them so everybody in the harbour would not see she was going down the road with an armload of shavings.

From Aspel Harbour to Spur Cove took twenty minutes to walk. When you passed the Silvers' house with the garden full of plum trees and reached the hilltop, you were out of Aspel Harbour: you saw Spur Cove and farther away the white church of Fox Cove. The only person who lived on the hill was the hermit. Marianne looked up at his house to see if there was any sign he was as crazy as people hinted: his curtains were drawn. She shouldn't have stopped: his door opened and he came out, waved.

"You're the girl from town … you're in the Devlins' old place."

"Yes …"

"The writer."

"Well … I'm trying to …"

"Marion." He said it the Irish way. "Come up, girl, I want a word with you."

He sat her at his table, which he'd set for his own tea. He gave her a small plate, a cup and saucer. On the plastic cloth he laid a clean cup towel, and on that a plate of jam-jams and slices of bread and margarine. He urged her to eat but did not eat anything himself. A pack of Rothmans lay beside his cup. Through his muslin curtains filtered sunlight in a waxy glow: it highlighted the puff of skin that stood out under his right eye like a cluster of miniature grapes, and rimmed the eye itself in a thin line of silver. Marianne was dying to pee.

"I have no toilet. There's a bucket." He led her to a closet where a pail stood. The roll of toilet paper stood on a kerosene drum. A fragment of a pair of men's thermal underpants hung on the rafters, stretched out over nails. She squatted over the pail.

When she returned he began a long story about the ancestry of his two dogs. A beam from the southwest window shone through the shell of his ear and illumined it bright red. He poured tea from a dipper on a two-burner hotplate.

"My rangette has two burners like that," she said. "But it has a small oven too. I like baking bread."

"I bake a scattered few loaves." It hadn't occurred to her that he could bake in his woodstove in the adjacent room. "Oh yes, don't be surprised. Last year I had thirteen Christmas cakes in here." The unlikely cakes popped into her view like magic, superimposed over the jam-jams, his daybed with its mustard coloured mandala-covered coverlet, the little shelf in the corner behind his television, the blue and golden flowered linoleum … ·

"Iced," he said.

"With marzipan?"

"No, not the yellow. White, I use. What you call hard icing. Thirteen cakes I had in here. And do you know I never sold one?"

"You had them for sale?"

"It cost me eighteen dollars to make each one, and I was charging twenty. For my time, you know. I sat by the woodstove and watched them so they wouldn't burn. And no one would look at them." He sat up, hands clasped on the table, his hairline straight as a doll's, his nose wide and soft, the grape cluster standing out beneath his runny eye with its liquid, gleaming rim. What had been wrong with the cakes? Marianne's view of them changed. The cakes looked decrepit now. They began to match more closely the mood of their environment. Some of the cherries were falling out. If you looked closely you saw in the cakes pieces of things that should not have been there; potato peel, sawdust, a carrot top.

"Where did you learn how to bake?"

"By gorr, now that's a hard thing to say. I learned a bit of cooking home with my sisters, but it wasn't until I was a cook on the boats that I really learned."

"The boats?"

"I worked on a boat taking fish to Brazil. On the way home we stopped to take on rum in Trinidad and the ship's cook disappeared. The crew drew matches out of the first engineer's hat. I drew the broken one. When we reached home I left that ship and got a berth on another one and by gorr before that one got to Trinidad the cook died. So I took it on again and I was a cook for fifteen years."

"You were destined to be a cook."

"There was a man came in last year when I had the cakes here, and by gorr he had only three months to live. And he was living on baby food, you know, that's all he could eat. You know the baby food out of jars."

"Mashed carrots…"

"You eat it with a spoon."

"Puréed peas…"

"And the like, yes, and when he came in here he said Ralph, I've got three months left to live and I've come for a slice," he said, "just a slice, mind, of your Christmas cake. So I gave him a cake and he went home and he wrapped it and put it under the tree, and on Christmas morning when the kids had unwrapped all their presents he unwrapped the Christmas cake, his wife told me later, Bertha, and he cut himself a slice this big…" He intersected his forefinger with another finger, "and he put it in his mouth. Well, he kept it in his mouth and he chewed it for an hour, and then he swallowed it. And he said that's it now, that's that, and I'm glad to get that, and he never said another word about cake."

Ralph lit a cigarette, went into a bedroom and came out with a framed photograph: his niece, her husband and little girl Josie, grown up now in medical school in Toronto. Marianne could not see their faces until she'd rubbed the grime off the glass.

"You never married?" she said.

"Not yet," he looked at her meaningfully, took the photograph back to its place and sat in his chair.

She reached for her scarf.

"That curtain," he pointed, "do you know why I put that there?"

"So people on the road can't see in?"

"There was a young girl used to come here once. To clean up. Then someone told her mother she was always over here. And I never saw her again. You understand."

"People interfere." Marianne had her coat on by now. She stood, and he got up beside her. She reached for the door.

"I've locked that door so no one can come in."

The hook had been fitted into its eye. She lifted it out. As she did so, he put his face against hers and gave her a gentle hug. His grizzles prickled her cheek.

"Next time you pass by come in and see me again. I'm always here." He said this last sentence looking her straight in the eye, his hand on her arm.

She delicately disengaged.

"That last girl," he said, "received twenty dollars a visit."

She forgot Mrs. Ruby's bag of shavings on his floor and when she got halfway down his path he came out, holding it outstretched, and when she reached for it he held on a second longer than needed, but he let go and she was free again, on the road away from his house, and did not look back, though she knew he stood there. Around the bend she felt relief to have escaped. Alders full of snowbirds lined the road, then thick grew the spruce and fir. There were little hiding places in the thickets; places where secret boulders for sitting on lay in mounds of emerald moss, and very small glades where you could listen to snowbird songs, and where different kinds of bushes grew, like the flame tree that had fiery leaves all summer and autumn and lay now in a crowd of tumbling branches that had the colour of the leaves in them, but muted so you could hardly see it.

On the hill's seaward side rose a funny, cleared hump with a few short spruce dotted on it like children playing *Mother May I*; motionless only because you were looking. Marianne looked away so they could move again, then whirled back on them. But they were too clever to let her catch them. They were good.

She remembered to look at the rose and its bud that had cracked into existence on the road. Near them lay a giant upturned root, like a crazy sun-wheel. There was Mrs. Ruby's house, across the road. Marianne saw no smoke—was she in?

You had to go around the back since they closed the store down. Over the gate to Walter's cabbage garden ran a clothesline with cup towels on it. The store sign lay near the back door: *Ruby's Store* painted in black and green. It looked too new to be lying on the ground, the paint twinkling. Marianne knocked. A huge cat hunched on the gatepost, motionless. The head of Mrs. Ruby peeped around the door; scrawny, curious and bedraggled as a murre hatchling.

"Are you not up yet, Mrs. Ruby?"

"Yes child, we're up, come in. What were you doing over in Ralph Carlyle's house?"

"How did you …"

"Never mind, come in, child." Mrs. Ruby wore a bright yellow blouse with black and brown zigzags that looked like buildings falling down. Walter sat at the table eating a chicken leg. The kitchen was full of cooking smells, the woodstove crackling and throwing waves of heat. Leo, the grown son, fried fish and onions in a cast iron pan.

"I've brought you a few shavings …"

"Well look, would you believe it, Walter, what the girl has brought, and her with no way of getting wood." She flung the shavings on top of her woodpile without ceremony.

Walter, thin and ancient, appraised the armload. "Good splits they are, too." He returned to his drumstick.

"Yes, very good ones they are too," parroted Mrs. Ruby. She brushed her hair at the mirror by the back door and it was as if a dandelion clock had brushed its fluff. Then she took a mop leaning in a corner, threw a teacup of water over it, and mopped a spot on the floor, sending bread crusts clattering. Marianne had never seen anyone mop a floor with a cup of water, and looked to see if this act surprised Walter, but it did not.

"We're waiting for Sister Jean to come from town with the laundry. Here, Walter, take that off—you don't want Sister

Jean to see that dirty old thing." Mrs. Ruby brought an Adidas sweatshirt out of another room. "Put this on." She rived his sweater off and pulled the new shirt over his head.

Once it was on, he kept being startled by the three white stripes down the sleeves. "I keep thinking," he confided to Marianne, "they're on the floor."

Mrs. Ruby spied the pan of fish and onions crackling on the stove without Leo, who'd gone upstairs.

"He goes up and leaves the pan on!" She thudded over to shake it around with a knife. It sizzled loud. The pieces of fish shone in chunks from the dark thickness of the pan. "Come look at the new calendar in the mail from Sister Jean's friend Sister Amelia in Ecuador. Marianne, come over, look!" Illustrated Bible stories. Moses and the burning bush. Jesus alone and palely loitering in limpid gardens, his beard ethereal. A verse on the back said take life one trial at a time.

"People had whiskers all over their faces at one time," said Walter. "All you could see was a bit here and here," he pointed at two spots above his cheekbones, "and their two eyes. Dirty-looking."

Mrs. Ruby made a quick pounce at him across the table. "Don't go saying that, Walter. Her boyfriend has a whisker." Her eyes were bright for battle.

"I'm not saying they should do anything about it or that it's right or wrong. I'm just saying they had them like that, the whiskers. And it's dirty-looking."

"He's only got a small moustache," Marianne interjected. She felt inadequate. Mrs. Ruby started talking about her other new calendar, hung over the stove, from her son in Norway. Ice, snow, coloured wooden houses.

"No different from here," ventured Marianne.

"Sure 'tis no different from here," Mrs. Ruby snapped at Marianne's sentence like a trout at a worm then spat it back.

She monitored the window for signs of weather, on account of Sister Jean navigating the roads. "Come over and look," she told Marianne. "See how it's coming over that dip in the mountains." Marianne looked out at a silkscreen of wooded hills dark in the foreground but becoming whiter with each hill. Soon the whiteness drew close, huge flakes nosing up to the steamed-up window like white moths.

"You hang your cup towels," complained Mrs. Ruby, "and expect them to blow fresh, but the line comes down a bit and that old tomcat, look, rubs and rubs himself all over them. Here..." she gave Marianne tea in a new gold-rimmed china cup out of the good cabinet in the other room, and thrust slices of homemade bread toasted on the woodstove. "And cake, I've only got this bit left over from Christmas..." a thin piece, spiced and fragrant.

"Mr. Carlyle, the man who lives by himself, he..." Marianne wanted to ask about his thirteen Christmas cakes, but Mrs. Ruby interrupted.

"What in the name of God do you want to be tangled up with him for? Gerald—tell her."

"Leave the girl alone, Margaret. Let her visit whoever she wants."

"Talk about dirty-looking! It's a wonder he never..." but the door blew open and Sister Jean came carrying bags with coat-hanger hooks sticking out of their tops and the bundle somehow took up half the kitchen. She gave Marianne a conspiratorial look—Mrs. Ruby is *old* but we are not—but Marianne did not want to become part of the conspiracy.

"I'd better go," she got up.

"Child," protested Mrs. Ruby, "you're welcome as the flowers in May..." but the protest was a ritual. The kitchen was too full. It was bursting with heat and laundry and the kind of trivial, pent-up arguments that scurry under kitchen tables and hide behind the tea tin and the biscuit box. Mrs. Ruby ducked behind the door that led into what used to be her old shop and came out with a plastic bag knotted at the top and bulging with tins and boxes. "Here," she slid it across the floor to Marianne.

"What's in it?"

"We'll talk about it later. Go on."

On the road, in the falling snow, she peeked in through the knot. Spaghetti, beans, a jar of strawberry jam, and something else, rolled up ... Marianne unfurled a corner and looked into the blue eyes of Jesus on Sister Amelia's calendar from Ecuador.

She took the shortcut through a field littered with mussel and winkle shells and crusts of urchins upturned like cups and full of meltwater reflecting the sky. She imagined beaks drinking from them. One tree grew in the field: the blackest spruce in the cove. In summer you always saw Ezekiel Vardy's black pony standing under the boughs. The spruce looked lonesome without the pony. She climbed over the fence and navigated the crumbling bank to the stony beach.

The beach was all green glass globules, polished, and mother-of-pearl cracked in winter, and magic lantern figurines made of bits of fish spine—the vertebrae. She slipped shells and bones in her gloves and climbed the boat-littered wharf, past the shredded flag in the yard of a new bungalow in whose driveway two men were fixing a truck. The flag had half its maple leaf when she moved here last spring. Now the leaf was gone, and so was all the white part. All that was left were shreds of the red bar close to the pole, and the red had faded to pink.

"Been shopping down on the beach," one of the men observed.

"Yes. Lots of bargains down there."

"How's Tom's place? That old roof hasn't fallen in on you yet? Marion, isn't it?"

"Marianne, yes."

"Well girl, if you need a few shingles nailed on, give us a call."

"Thanks."

"Remember that, now. Don't be a stranger."

Hens pecked around his boots. A soot-black rooster with a scarlet comb strutted resplendent in the snow. Farther up the hill glowed the dormant flame tree. It made Marianne think of the burning bush page in her new calendar. Snow had settled in white fingers over the fingers of the roadside spruce and fir, an endless pattern of shapes like hands; white snow-fingers settled against dark spruce and fir fingers; hands on hands—the trees' only chance to be caressed all over—how they must love it.

The headlands had turned white and reflected beams of white light on the calm sea. All the fence posts were edged in a soft white layer like icing, and whiteness filled the air. Everything was still. She came up over the hilltop and stopped in the road.

My smoke is white.

Her fire, burning in her absence with Ezekiel's birch and her dry kindling, rose thick and pure white, into the cove's own whiteness. Her smoke had never done this. Now hers was no different from her neighbours'. As thick as the smoke of the Silvers next door was hers, which until today had made a pathetic trail next to the Silvers' thick, proud plume.

Her gloves' fingers were full of bits of shell and bone. It was hard to hold Mrs. Ruby's shopping bag. She knew exactly where to hang her new calendar: the same place Mrs. Ruby hung hers, up over the woodstove looking down on the kitchen. She headed for home and her underwear drawer where she kept her two-inch nails and a small hammer, and marvelled at this day that had decided to let her in, when it could have lowered the latch on its gull-white door and quietly turned her away.

The Christmas Room

"Come down," Mrs. Halloran begged Marianne, "and give me a hand with my wallpaper." A rule of the cove was that you had to redo all your walls before Christmas, either with a new coat of paint from Lundrigans or with wallpaper.

This would be the second Christmas since Mrs. Halloran's husband Leonard had died. He'd lifted one end of a two-by-four to be sawn for the new McDonalds in St. John's, and he'd had a massive heart attack. Marianne, sitting on her picnic table playing her guitar, saw the priest get out of a maroon limousine. He was not the local priest but came from down the shore. He looked like a skeleton. Mrs. Halloran had been baking three lemon meringue pies, and they burnt black.

"I was going to bring you up a bit," she'd told Marianne, "but now I don't know when I'll ever get to bake them again. I may never bake another lemon pie. I made them for him. He loved them." The following October Marianne had come from a walk to the pond and found a wedge of lemon pie quivering on her kitchen table.

But these days Mrs. Halloran wore her blue sweater with rust-coloured stripes and blotches of paint on its elbows. Every day she put on her black pants that had grown patches of knobbles. She no longer combed her hair except when she went to mass and bingo, and her perm stood in little periscopes that had corners instead of curls. There were pieces of wallpaper caught in it now. Leaning against the couch, amid scraps and curls of wallpaper, was a garbage bag full of Christmas presents.

Even after two years here, Marianne was not sure how Mary and Margaret and Mary-Margaret and the other old women of the cove viewed Mrs. Halloran, but she had an idea that Mrs. Halloran lived differently from the others, and that it had something to do with ambition and money and maybe pride. Nothing could have induced any of the Marys or Margarets, for instance, to go out on the main road on a frosty night in a headscarf and rubber boots, and hitchhike to bingo in Admirals Cove. This was a thing Mrs. Halloran did regularly in the hope of winning enough to get her to Florida again, as she had done after her jackpot ten years ago. The other women did not appear to have more money than Mrs. Halloran had, but they kept old ways that meant they did not need as much, whereas Mrs. Halloran uttered a never-ending lament about all the things she wanted but could not have: modern things one bought in the new superstores on the outskirts of St. John's. Marianne's house was behind Mrs. Halloran's, and Mrs. Halloran did not keep the distance from Marianne and her city ways that the other women kept, so Marianne found herself in Mrs. Halloran's orbit more often than she herself might have arranged. She had come here to live after a joyride with a friend who was a painter, a visit during which the red willows and foam-drenched bird islands had seduced her into fleeing the city and renting a fisherman's house in the cove. This land responded, she thought, it leant toward you and if it did not exactly talk to you it confided something, and offered a surprising level of companionship like a trustworthy person who did not rattle on about trivialities. Even now, as the cove prepared for Christmas, its green meadows retained a bright and profound glow as from lit cloth.

"You have lots of shopping done," Marianne said, eyeing the bag of presents that rested on the couch near a pair of giant swans, hoping the topic might lift the sorrowful little hoods over Mrs. Halloran's eyes, but it did not.

"Laura have all those presents bought," said Mrs. Halloran. Laura was her daughter. She was in town for the day with her husband Stuart and their little girl, Patty. "I have none. Not a one. Can't get to do anything. I've no money. That's all I can do about it."

The giant swans were made of brittle plastic that came from the 1950s before anyone knew how to make plastic supple. The plastic was black, the molded feathers sprayed gilt. Under the swans lay a pair of landscapes, each with a white cloud, a caribou moss foreground and glitter-topped mountains with trees made of real birch bark. Against these leaned Saint Anne holding the infant Virgin Mary, a sacred heart of Jesus, a photograph of clipper ships in Boston harbour, and a school photograph of Mrs. Halloran's foster son Jody, clasping a captain's wheel. From the couch cushions dangled a board decorated with nails in the shape of a bridge, silver thread strung from nail to nail, glorious like the Golden Gate, except for a dubious area near the bottom where thread had escaped the general symmetry and gone meandering around the wrong nails. Pinned to it a red rosette proclaimed First Prize. Some teacher in Fox Cove School must assign a similar project every year, Marianne thought, because everyone had one somewhere in the house. She had also seen the Railway Engine, the Airplane, and the Ship.

The wall over the couch remained covered in paper that had brown, orange and cream stripes, and so did the window wall facing the islands. The wall with the door in it had been newly papered, but the fourth wall fascinated Marianne.

"No money for nothing now around here, supposing I was to sell my own bedclothes and dishes," said Mrs. Halloran with great pathos. "I've a mind to call up Junior Etcheverry and take him up on his offer to sell him my sods."

"Your sods?"

"The sods over there on Leonard's bit of meadow he used to graze his horse on." She nodded past the curtains toward the headland that spoke daily to Marianne, where early winter sun lit the russet sorrel.

"The grass?"

"I'm already after selling his horse, and that money is spent. I wonder would Leonard come down from heaven and murder me? Supposing heaven's where he is, and not … Jesus, Mary and Joseph what kind of badness do I be thinking about my own husband … I can't be selling his sods. There's a thing Leonard never would have allowed."

Marianne suspected Leonard had forbidden lots of things that were done here now with festive zeal. She watched Mrs. Halloran unroll and match a length of paper with the last piece she had hung. Before her listlessness, Mrs. Halloran had possessed a lovely smile. Now her eyes were always wet. She was too young to get the Canada pension. Laura had just given up her job selling Avon because they'd wanted her to hurry too much. Stuart had a heart condition and payments to make on the car. He could not shovel snow or lift anything.

"Do you mean you can sell grass off a meadow?" Marianne had not heard of such a thing. Was it, she wondered, like the woman in the O. Henry story who sold her luxuriant hair?

"Jody wants a snowsuit for Christmas. He needs one. I'm after putting two loads of his clothes in the dryer today where he was in the woods and came home soaked to the skin."

Mrs. Halloran folded the length of wallpaper where it met the ceiling and tore a notch near the skirting board. She sliced it with a knife that had a bone handle and a crescent blade, and dipped the cut piece in the bucket of warm paste Marianne had carried from the kitchen. Together they smoothed the paper over the former layer of velvet paper, which sopped up the paste and showed through the orange blossoms. Mrs. Halloran stood on a chair and cut surplus paper with a pair of scissors she said wouldn't cut butter in July. Marianne had no wallpapering experience. The fourth wall was half covered in rough green paper with a smooth gold pattern of zigzags and pagodas. Another strip—not the brown, orange and cream stripes, and not the new wallpaper all cream with orange blossoms, and not the velvet wallpaper—revealed green and violet windmills. The rest of the fourth wall was covered in a sheet of false brick facade.

"Laura bought that brick board when I was away this summer. I don't like it a bit. It cost forty-six dollars a sheet. I'll have to get the hammer now, and get those nails out ... Jody!"

Jody had come in from the woods and sat in the living room eating a bag of chips and watching a movie about American soldiers in Vietnam.

"If you believe in bad luck," the commander told his soldiers, "that's what you're going to get." The commander was noble and flinty and the soldiers were going to be transformed by him in the next two hours into heroes, whereas now they were cowards and children.

"What, Mom?"

"Where's the hammer?"

"I don't know!"

"You don't know nothing, you don't."

"What?"

"Never mind, I'll get it myself."

"Mom, what's wrong with you?"

Mrs. Halloran pried out the finishing nails. Marianne picked more nails off the carpet. "Stuart left those there when they were putting this up," Mrs. Halloran said. "Now where are we going to lay this? ... Jody!"

"What?"

"Come here 'til I asks you."

"What do you want?" He stood in the doorway.

"Where am I supposed to lay this to?" She stood with a sheet of the faux brick facade.

"I don't know. The shed's blocked and the door's frozen. Can't you lay it down in the room somewhere 'til I finds a place for it tomorrow?'

"No, I cannot."

"What about the room where you keep the sawdust?" Marianne said. That room was off the porch. The sawdust cost a dollar a sack at the sawmill. Mrs. Halloran used it as litter for her eight cats.

"I don't know what about that," said Mrs. Halloran.

"She's blocked as well," Jody said.

But Mrs. Halloran lifted the huge sheet through the doorway anyway. Marianne helped. They put it in the sawdust room, between Jody's bike and the tool bench.

The removal of the false bricks exposed other wallpaper edges at the end of the adjoining wall, like pages of a book. Marianne counted nine, and beyond that her fingers could not reach.

"What this room really wants is wallboard," Mrs. Halloran measured a new piece of orangeblossom paper, "to make it level. I'll put some up next winter if I live that long, please God." Marianne saw all down the years, Christmas after Christmas, layer after layer, until Mrs. Halloran stood in the centre of a Christmas room hardly any bigger than herself, putting up new wallpaper. Then Mrs. Halloran would have to lose weight so she could fit into the Christmas room, to paper it. She would go on a diet, and she would get smaller and smaller, until finally she would turn into the caraway seed in the centre of a jawbreaker.

And the jawbreaker would not go unsucked. Obviously there was an insatiable beast of some kind, because the Christmas room of Mrs. Halloran was not the only one of its kind in the harbour. The shore was full of houses that had rooms in them that were just like Mrs. Halloran's Christmas room. And it wasn't just the Christmas rooms either. As Mrs. Halloran wetted the orangeblossom wallpaper, she was waiting for banana-coloured paint on the bottom half of her kitchen walls to dry, and the top half was covered in wallboard Laura had just painted white since the brown looked too dingy. Across the road, at Thomas and Mary's, they were waiting for Harold Luby to come over with his sparkle gun to fire sparkles over the swirls of stucco his brother Stephen had applied with a trowel the previous week. Mary was trying to get her family to let her get red and silver sparkles this time. Over at Marg and Alfie's next to Thomas and Mary's, they were putting new canvas on the kitchen floor and tiles on the hall ceiling. And once everything was done, the talk would be of what really should have been done, and what should be done as soon as possible to perfect things. Satisfaction was always just a sheet of aspenite out of reach. Or a sheet of floor canvas, a roll of carpet, a roll of wallpaper, a length of molding, or some Barker tile. It was always something found in sheets, preferably sheets that could be rolled up; that was the missing link between the women of the shore and happiness. Marianne decided it was because you could afford a sheet of wallboard or a roll of wallpaper, whereas you might not be able to afford the beautiful homes that appeared on television, especially the soap operas, where faucets were solid brass, bathtubs were oval and embossed with lilies.

The women of the shore did not go outside except to hang their washing, go to mass, or get groceries. So they did not see the wildflowers Marianne saw. New wildflowers appeared all spring and summer long, until by August there were wild roses, yellow wild peas, blue wild peas, forget-me-nots, chuckley pear flowers, and, in Marianne's garden, her favourite flower, sweet william. Could Mrs. Halloran really mean to sell the grass and all its little wildflowers off her dead husband's meadow?

"I might go over after we're finished this," Marianne said, "and pick some of the sorrel on Leonard's meadow, if you don't mind."

"Sorrel?"

"It's a wild plant. The leaves are pointy with two spurs. I put it in soup. It adds a sour taste." Putting wild plants in food was something Marianne knew set her apart as a bit of a wing nut in the cove. But she'd been looking at the sorrel and thinking how it had grown, and now if someone was going to somehow take away the grass...

"Sour? Them tall ones with the heads you can rub apart like red powder?"

"Yes."

"Sallysuckers, we called them, when we were young. We didn't put them in any soup though. We ate them out of our hands. Hungry, we'd devour anything. We were never in the house in those days, even when we were older, fifteen, sixteen, seventeen. Even for awhile after we all got married. I don't know what happened to us."

"You and Mary and Margaret?"

"Outdoors all the time, yes. Myself and Mary and Marg. With our bamboo fishing poles. We'd go to Spur Cove Pond and we'd get the biggest kind of trout. One summer Mary and Marg were both pregnant. I used to have to climb up in the trees to fetch their hooks. We were different then. We're all big now. Skinny? How skinny were we, especially Mary, and you know how big she is now. I brought a baking powder cake one day, a great big one, and Mary sat by the pond and ate that whole cake. I didn't want any. But she could eat the works. My what a laugh we'd have then, the three of us in at that pond, with me crawling around up in the trees."

Mrs. Halloran took herself back so easily to happier times that in a minute she was no longer depressed but laughing like a girl. Marianne wanted to hug her. Someone had always looked after her. Now she had no one, and she was getting old, and she wasn't used to it. She needed someone she could depend on, and Marianne knew she was not the right person, and felt inadequate. But Mrs. Halloran seemed to consider Marianne sufficient as a friend all the same, and she trusted her. The sea was sucking the beach; Marianne could see it out Mrs. Halloran's new white window with the twelve small panes. Maybe the sea was the insatiable beast responsible for all the wallpaper and floor canvas and sparkly stucco ceilings. But you couldn't even blame the sea, really, thought Marianne. What hunger made the sea need to suck? Greed wasn't a thing that had a human origin. Hunger and need were in the air. The bees would gorge sweetness out of the red and white clover until their bellies distended. Everything urged its need, need, need, like the song of the wedding-bird in spring. The secret, Marianne wondered, the secret had something to do with not fearing the need. Because the fear was, you wouldn't be able to feed the need, and because you did not have food for it, it would devour you.

"Feed the need, feed the need, feed the need, don't fear it," Marianne could hear the wedding-bird singing. And she thought of Mrs. Ruby down the road, and knew Mrs. Ruby fed everything that asked her to, and always had enough, and put new paint and paper on her walls once a year in time for Christmas, no fooling around, and that need was fed and that was the end of it. Marianne wondered what was the difference between Mrs. Ruby and Mrs. Halloran, because she knew Mrs.

Ruby was fearless though Walter Ruby had died, and Mrs. Halloran had always been afraid, even before Leonard had died. There were the rooms, and the wallpaper, and the sea, sucking and needing, and beyond that were storms and piles of clouds and the sun and moon. Mrs. Ruby had told Marianne she admired how smart God must be to know exactly when to send down the first snow every year, and from the way she said it, Marianne could see Mrs. Ruby imagined God's snow all stockpiled in a special area up among certain clouds in the highest parts of the sky. God. Maybe Mrs. Ruby had made a bargain with God. I'll feed everything that comes here hungry, God, and you make sure there's enough. I won't worry if you send the supplies. Maybe the need had grown so insistent that Mrs. Ruby had made that bargain, since she could meet the need in no other way. And maybe Mrs. Halloran still thought she had to meet the need personally herself, out of store-houses of food and supplies that she knew she did not possess. Marianne wished she could tell Mrs. Halloran to lay all her troubles at God's feet, but of course she could not do that, because in her own soul the great maw of the sea, the open beak of the wedding-bird, and her own empty womb were cry-ing, "Need, need, need," with a din and a clatter that Marianne couldn't quiet down long enough to get a message through to the one with whom all things were possible for those who believed. The most she could do was invite Mrs. Halloran to come to mass with her. She did not normally go to mass her-self, and was not even Roman Catholic, but liked to sit under the great rose window and let the green saints and their lambs and lilies descend in a sunbeam and float across the skin of her arms, and she liked the hum and drone of the women of the cove saying their rosary like bees among the cove's roses.

"No, I won't go today." Mrs. Halloran held up a strip of dripping orangeblossom paper. "I've got to get this one wall finished. You should bring me a bulletin. Jody always forgets to bring me one."

The bulletin was green. It had the bingo times on it. When Marianne brought it to Mrs. Halloran she found Laura and Jody and Mrs. Halloran arguing how to measure carpet for the pantry floor. The carpet was thick and dusty—someone had given them it. She had to step over rolls of it piled in the kitchen. The pantry floor was cold, since they had ripped its canvas off. Mrs. Halloran thanked Marianne for the bulletin. Before Marianne left she saw that a green bulletin lay on top of the television in the living room, because this time Jody had remembered to bring one home. It was like that with everything Marianne tried to do to help. She was not needed, not really, not in any way that might last.

The next morning a horrendous clattering woke her before 7:30. She looked out her bedroom window and saw a man riding some sort of tractor over Mrs. Halloran's meadow, slicing lengths of sod off it, and in some mysterious way rolling as it sliced, so the entire meadow was stripped and littered with what looked like the cakes Marianne's mother used to call Swiss rolls. But they were not made of sponge cake and jam, but of the beautiful grass of the field, and the man, Junior Etcheverry, had a helper hoisting them onto a flatbed truck to be taken to some housing development that was probably not far from where Leonard Halloran had suffered his heart attack.

Now Mrs. Halloran could pay, Marianne remembered, for Jody's snowsuit. Or could she? There were so many things Mrs. Halloran wanted. Maybe the sods would metamorphose into a big new TV, or an exercise bike, or a microwave for Jody to heat up Pizza Pockets after school. There was Mrs. Halloran now, waving up at Marianne's window, lifting four triumphant fingers and shouting something. Marianne opened her window.

"Four hundred dollars!" Marianne barely heard this over the racket of Junior's sod cutter. "I'll be able to rip down all that old wallpaper and put in brand new wallboard!"

There was something unbearable, Marianne felt, about bartering the earth's green coverlet for boards to line Mrs. Halloran's Christmas room. Yet she knew Mrs. Halloran might never again have to worry about layers of wallpaper that peeled and deteriorated, or grew out of fashion, or reminded her of the years when her husband had called all the shots, and what was wrong with that? Marianne wished she could flee in her bathrobe across the road to Mary's or Margaret's house, to get them on the meadow's side, to fight for the outdoors they'd loved before they married and had children and changed the wallpaper over and over again to make up for the purple daisies, red clover, buttercups and Queen Anne's lace on which they had turned their backs, but would they know what she was on about?

Marianne had not lived her whole life in the cove as they had done. She had not galloped to school with them on a horse, had not devoured cake with them by the trout pond while Mrs. Halloran climbed overhead searching for lost lures. Marianne murmured no rosary in blessed light from a rose window. Her well had shrews drowned in it and she was foolish enough to strain them out and drink the water. She threw sallysuckers in her soup, and one day she would take off with that weekend boyfriend of hers with the silken hands, and would resume the life she had left in the city for this borrowed bit of cove life. She sensed her mourning for the torn and sold meadow marked her every bit as lost as Mrs. Halloran would appear once the sod money was spent, caught in a stranger's headlights in the snow, beseeching him to drive her to bingo, and she shut her bedroom window and did not try to save anything.

Every Waking Moment

"The Worship Centre welcomes you downtown." Black letters on mango-coloured poster paper. They were up all along Duckworth Street, on telephone poles and in store windows. Marianne ripped one off the green wooden doors of Tom Callahan: Novelties, Gifts, Tobacconist, which had closed down three years ago.

> "TO HEAR: TO ENJOY: TO CONSIDER: TO RECEIVE: God's Word of Love—Special Music & Congregational Sing-ing—Living Testimonies—Fellowship. SUNDAY EVENINGS 6:30pm January 24, 31. February 7, 14. FREE ADMISSION. At Belle Isle "B" Ballroom Rubicon Plaza Hotel 160 New Spencer Street. IF YOU NEED—Transportation—Prayer/Counsel-ling—Information CALL 268-1883, 765-4708, 592-3397. Pastors Kevin Woolridge, Don Maynard."

At the top of the poster had been drawn a stylized dove and cross. At the bottom was an ornate R in a circle, the logo of the Rubicon Hotel. The Rubicon was new. Reflected in its shining walls were the brine-worn facades of saddleries, ware-houses and pubs across New Spencer Street. Marianne had never been in there, but she had hitched a ride once from Aspel Harbour to town with Rose, who had a new job there as a room service maid. Rose had been looking forward to meeting the important guests who would, the management told her, be coming. They would tip well. Before the place opened there had been a dinner for the staff and local dignitaries like the premier. There had been a gelatin salmon with a real salmon suspended in it, with mint leaves down the middle and devilled eggs with blue food colouring in the yolks down the sides. There had been rehearsals for staff members before the hotel opened. Rose had had to take trays of tea and coffee and baskets of fruit and steaming tureens up the elevator and along the corridors without taking too long and without spilling anything. She told Marianne there hadn't been enough rehearsals and she was nervous. The hotel had been opening the day Marianne hitched the ride.

The poster had the initials P.A.O.N. in fine print at the bottom. Marianne knew that meant it came from the Pentecostals. Her family was not Pentecostal. Her brother, the one like Burt Reynolds, had gone out with Pentecostal girls. They had been clean and pretty, and they had studied French and been intelligent. Marianne's brother was too wild for them, and they had each married someone else.

The Pentecostals were pretty crazy. Everyone knew that. But Marianne wanted to go. She wanted TO HEAR: TO ENJOY: TO CONSIDER: TO RECEIVE: God's Word of Love, the special music and singing, and the fellowship. She could do without the living testimonies, but she was hungry for the rest, because all her searching through sacred teachings of the east and the west had led her to this street, and to this orange poster. The Anglican Cathedral up the road had a museum in it. In the museum was the skeleton of a church mouse from Westminster Abbey. The skeleton was dark brown with holes in it, and to Marianne that skeleton was the same as the cathedral: dark, with holes, dead, and scary. When she went in one day to sit and be quiet, the vicar came up and asked her if anything was the matter, then some cleaners came in and plugged in an industrial vacuum cleaner that made a great noise. Sometimes the cathedral door was locked and you had to ring the bell. On Sundays the services were attended by one or two dozen ancient immigrants from Gloucester and Kent. The sermons were about church hierarchy and points of order, and there were prayers for the continued glory of the Queen.

The doors of the Roman Catholic basilica were always open. But she couldn't get inside that place either, not like people born and steeped in it. She visited its altar and ate the body of Christ fraudulently, and wondered if anyone spied her. Mrs. Ruby from Aspel Harbour and her daughter, Sister Jean, sometimes came here. Imagine if they saw Marianne eating the body of Christ. She had eaten it once in Aspel Harbour when her friend Tim came to visit and brought her to the service with him—he'd broken his host and sneaked half of it back to their pew, and had given it to her to eat. The Catholics did not give you wine—the priest drank it all.

She folded the mango-coloured poster and slid it between her driver's permit and her library card. She told Tim and Lloyd she was going, but didn't tell Lloyd it was the Pentecostals. Lloyd had been her lover for four years and this was the last thing he needed to know. He was tolerant of all her yogis and books about Zen, her Hindu scriptures and her vegetarianism that began one day after she'd devoured a whole chicken for lunch.

He had not liked the appearance of the Bible or the table with candles and flowers on it. "It looks like an altar," he said. "It makes me sick… I've had enough of plastic Jesus and Hail Mary and Jesuit fathers being hauled in for gross indecency." But he loved Marianne. He'd find a way to put up with this.

Lloyd lived on a long street in town. The street had a vanishing point. It had telephone poles and wires that converged. It had cats on doorsteps, ragamuffin children, and sunshine spilling over the roofs. It had chimneys. It had St. Hilda's Hospital at the end, looking, at sunset, like an adobe palace washed in rose and gold light. The Rubicon Hotel was beyond St. Hilda's. Marianne walked toward it on January 24th after the supper of halibut and roast potatoes with red skins and corn. Lloyd was a good cook. She'd made a salad with olive oil and garlic and lemon. The street was dark. It was raining. The streetlamps had silver lines streaming down to the dead flowerbeds at their bases. A sleek, wet German shepherd walked with Marianne, his fur soaking through her skirt to her leg, then he turned up Colonial Street, his claws clicking the pavement. Through Wing Garden Take-out's lit windows she saw two youths in jeans and red lumbershirts leaning on the counter waiting for their #2 combination plates. One was using the phone.

The houses were right on the sidewalk. Someone's curtains were open. Unused candlesticks on the mantelpiece; wallboard, photographs of people standing in front of artificial skies, a woman and man sitting in chairs in the light from their television. The man blowing blue smoke rings and knitting an Icelandic sweater. The woman sliding her fingers round a bowl on her chair-arm to get the last crumbs. The six o'clock news anchorman trapped in her spectacles.

The foghorn was lowing. Halley's Comet was somewhere up there but she had no chance of seeing it on a night like this. Through alleys downhill Marianne could see the harbour and all the lights. Whiffs of seaweed and whores'-egg scent blew uphill and caught her in the face.

The Rubicon had many entrances. Marianne followed her nose. The towers rose in black glass cubes into the sky. They were really part of Florida.

"Welcome to the worship centre," said a short, fat man in the doorway. Marianne kept moving as if she was on wheels. People filled rows of folding tin chairs; women sheathed in sheer dresses with glossy belts, pantyhose, makeup and perfume, their husbands in suits. They'd driven from the suburbs. But the back five rows held a few men who had straggled in from downtown alleys in wet coats and unlaced workboots. On a stage hung a banner bearing a dove and cross, and there was an overhead projector.

Someone sounded cymbals.

A man announced, "Greet your neighbour," and there was a swell of rising bodies shaking hands, coming too close. A woman, brittle and coiffed, hugged Marianne. The woman's dress was yellow with white snippets all over it in the shape of fingernail clippings. "You look familiar ... you're?"

"Marianne Cullen."

"You're from Poplar Dam."

"... A long time ago, yes."

"Well, I'm Doris Keys. I used to teach you skating when you were in grade five! You were *this* high. I thought you looked familiar ... *Dianne* ..." she called to her friend, "this is Marianne Cullen. I taught her skating when she was a child." Marianne thought Doris Keys looked too young to have done this, though she did look a bit embalmed. "Oh— the music—Marianne, we're all going to sing a few hymns of praise ..."

Words appeared on the screen. The hymns were not symmetrical. She liked their rhythm. She could get enthusiastic about singing them. The people at this meeting could harmonize and counterpoint. Some people hummed or clapped, and Marianne realized Doris Keys had begun whistling like a bird. There was passion in the music; voices escaped their owners and turned wild. The voices left the manicured, conventional bodies and flew all over the room until the entire place had cracked open.

Marianne was all in favour of breaking into song. She wondered why people did not do it every day, in ordinary situations, when something touched or moved them. Why did we all have voices if not to sing? Why not be exuberant, sometimes, and rejoice? Lloyd had chastised her about this just the other day, in Shelley's Diner: the tomato juice had shocked Marianne with its refreshing jolt; tart, red and cold.

"I love it," she'd enthused. "Who would have thought this little glass of red, almost brown, really... could be... it's so—*revitalizing.*"

Maybe she had said the word revitalizing a bit loud and maybe it was not the right kind of word to let people in Shelley's hear you utter, but Lloyd had glowered. "For god's sake, Marianne—it's only a glass of tomato juice." He hadn't understood. But these people, well, they understood something about bursting into song over some sort of glory, even if it was an unseen glory and had not come out of a Heinz tin.

Pastor Kevin Woolridge disentangled a snake of microphone wire with a flip of his hand. Cities, he said, and movies and lines of traffic and traffic lights and television sitcoms were not fulfilling the deep hunger in North America today: only Jesus could fill it.

Rosemary Stratton approached the microphone with her testimony, in a red dress. She had seen Billy Graham on television and this warm feeling had flowed through her whole body. "Yes, I'm here," said God. But her kidneys had hurt for years. She was afraid she would have to get hooked up to a machine. Then a revival crusade came to the stadium. There were tents up and everything. "Lord," said the evangelist. Not Billy Graham himself, but did that really matter? "There is someone here who has pain in the lower back.

Make them whole, in the name of Jesus." And the warm feeling had burned into her kidneys, and when the heat drained away the pain was gone. "And only Jesus can do that," said Rosemary. Only Jesus has the power to get right in there and heal those tissues."

Chris Warren came to the microphone. He reminded her of Lloyd, his neat moustache and ten extra pounds, which on Lloyd were irresistible. Three years ago, Chris Warren said, his life was an endless round of late-night drinking, smoking dope and doing things he didn't even want to mention here tonight. Then a friend invited him to church, and gradually...

The difference between Chris Warren and Lloyd, Marianne thought, besides the fact that Chris's flesh looked deadened while Lloyd's was clear and scattered with freckles that struck her as stars in the sky—she looked for constellations in Lloyd, and had found Orion and even the Seven Sisters, and some other constellations to be found nowhere in the real sky—the difference was what she might call a divide. There was a divide between these church people—if you could call this a church—and the glory they proclaimed. It was not in their bodies at all, but confined to what Pastor Kevin Woolridge was now calling the Holy Spirit, which did not appear to Marianne to have imbued these people with the life their pastor claimed it had. They all looked hammered and dulled to Marianne: someone had sprinkled a thin layer of dust on them. Many appeared to be dental hygienists or real estate agents during those hours when they were not raising their arms and singing in harmony about the risen lord. There was a divide in Lloyd as well, but Lloyd's was different. Of course she had never told him about the constellations she had found, or that she thought of his skin as a kind of sky. They had made love under a tree hung with apples in the moonlight on his parents' farm, and he'd kept his leather jacket on and she would always, she knew, remember the smell of that leather and the way the apples hung. The divide in Lloyd was not separation from an unseen glory, but simply his failure to be conscious of any ordinary loveliness in which he might be steeped at all times, in every waking moment...

The pastor was saying something about loneliness, and tears started running down Marianne's face and made her furious with herself, especially when Doris Keys the skating teacher came over and slipped her arm around Marianne's shoulder.

People raised their arms in the air and were swaying like trees. And some were murmuring things which were incomprehensible and which Marianne guessed were either in tongues or supposed to be in tongues.

Doris Keys' friend Dianne and another woman in a sea-green dress jittered over like bees. Doris bent and hugged Marianne. Marianne hugged her back. It felt like hugging a bag of crab shells.

Doris said, "I just knew when you came in tonight that you were hurting."

"You did?"

"Oh, honey, yes," said Doris Keys. "I looked at you and I just knew you really needed the Lord." Throughout the service, Marianne had heard Doris Keys sing in a clear-belled voice, harmony not melody, as she played with the hair of her husband, tall and handsome, his dark curls just beginning to turn grey. Their little girl, about seven, had clutched Doris's other hand.

"You need fellowship," said the woman in the sea-green dress. She scribbled on the back of her business card and gave it to Marianne. The card's front read;

HALCYON

Stephanie B. Munden

Life Underwriter

The Halcyon Assurance Company Limited

44 Haines Division Blvd., St. John's, Newfoundland A1C 4B9

Residence: (709) 592-2450   Office: (709) 765-4497

Marianne had stopped crying but now needed to blow her nose. Doris Keys gave her a tissue out of her pocket. She said it was slightly used but not too bad, then glanced over to where her handsome husband stood over a petite woman who wore a velvet band in her blonde hair. Marianne blew her nose on Doris's tissue. She saw a red stain on the tissue and hid it under her thumb, aghast that blood must have come out of her nose when she'd been blowing it. She crammed the tissue in her coat pocket. At the same moment, Doris's little girl emerged from the crowd.

"Mommy, can I go up to the top floor of the hotel and look out the window?'

"We have to go talk to Daddy. He's the one to ask about that."

"But Daddy's busy talking to Mrs. Pettigrew. He said..."

Doris's husband was indeed talking to Mrs. Pettigrew, bending over the velvet hairband while Mrs. Pettigrew laughed into his eyes. Doris Keys took her daughter's hand and excused herself somewhat abruptly, leaving Marianne with Stephanie Munden in her sea-green dress.

"Turn it over," Stephanie said. "Read the back."

On the back of her card Stephanie had written in flowing capitals with a fine-tip purple pen,

Marianne:

> *FOR GOD HAS NOT GIVEN ME*
> *THE SPIRIT OF FEAR, BUT OF*

*LOVE AND OF POWER AND OF
A SOUND MIND.*

1 Timothy

"The verse is no longer of much use to me," Stephanie Munden said, then leaned closer and whispered—"But it's my own fault. I can't do without *sex*. I've tried and I just can't, I'm too weak. But you—take that verse to heart, I promise it'll work. The Lord is real, and all-powerful, and He'll meet you where you have your greatest need. He tried to meet me, He really did, but I couldn't make the sacrifice. I'm weak, and I just love sex way too much…"

Marianne remembered hearing somewhere, maybe in the Anglican crypt, something about the word of god falling onto different kinds of ground, some fertile, others not. How much, she wondered, did Stephanie Munden love sex? Was she a woman whose appetite led her to pursue men on the street and arrange to have sex with them; strange men whom Stephanie did not even know—young, suit-clad workers at the new Toronto Dominion building, innocently carrying vinegar-stained packets along Water Street from the chip wagon on their lunch breaks, until… No, Stephanie had not meant that. Marianne remembered that these people, the Pentecostals, in fact did not or were not supposed to have sex unless they were married. Stephanie was, Marianne realized, a single woman, hardly older than herself… a normal woman, but one who believed she was somehow wrong to crave nakedness, body heat, or the salt lick of a lover's translucent skin, filled with stars.

Two nights later Marianne went to see a movie with Lloyd. There was no toilet paper in the cubicle at the cinema washroom. She took a tissue out of her pocket. She uncrumpled it and saw that the red stain was Doris Keys' lipstick. It was a perfect outline of Doris's open mouth, and it showed all the fullness and membranes of her lips like the segment of a juicy orange. It spoke to Marianne.

"Pentecostal women are very careful about keeping their husbands," it said. And then Marianne flushed it down the toilet, and went back to watch the movie with Lloyd. When it was over he asked if she wanted to drive outside town to see Halley's Comet.

"It's a clear night and you were saying you'd like to see it."

He drove her down the Southern shore in his cream-coloured Volkswagen and parked at the top of Tors Cove where an old lane with a wooden fence led over a hill and down to Hare's Ears beach. The comet was a blur, hardly illumined, a stain of milk spilled on a black coat and only half sunk in. The fact that it was a blur reminded her it was moving fast, though it appeared as at a standstill. She kept her eyes raised to it as they walked, linking her arm in Lloyd's and relying on him for direction, leaning on him; she did not need to look down at the lane. By the time they got down to the pebbles and the edge of the water, the hill's spruce silhouettes had angled to obscure the comet.

"That walk," she said, "was a once-in-a-lifetime happening."

"Was it?'

"Yes." Didn't he know Halley's Comet came only once about every seventy-five years? Unless they lived to be a hundred...

"Did you enjoy that?"

"I loved it."

"Would you like to do it again?"

He led her back up the hill, turned around where they'd begun, and together they walked all the way down the hill again, to the water and the stones. Neither spoke. It felt extravagant, as if Lloyd had really caused the comet to make its visitation twice in a lifetime instead of only once, through some miraculous intervention. It delighted her. Only later, as they lay tangled in his bed, did it occur to her to wonder whether Lloyd had bothered to look up at the comet at all.

PART TWO

THE FREEDOM IN AMERICAN SONGS

JENNIFER HAD BEEN AT KERRY to get rid of the antique gate in the garage for over twenty years. She was right. He knew she was—it was just that it was a beautiful gate—its sinuous garlands and lilies reminded him of the elfin grot in Keats' *La Belle Dame Sans Merci*—and he'd always imagined he might put it up at the entrance to their nonexistent country place, though he'd known the gate really belonged to something out of the last century, some humongous heap of a place in the rich part of town. It was outrageous, really, the size of it—Jennifer was right. And he had put ads in the paper and online, but he had never in a million years dreamed that who should come to see the gate but . . .

The visitor shook his hand and said, "Xavier, my name's Xavier Boland," and Kerry wondered if there could be more than one Xavier Boland, or if he had misheard the name.

Looking his visitor in the face he could not see the features of his old acquaintance, and the visitor made no intimation that he recognized Kerry at all. That was what happened, wasn't it? How many times had people from thirty-five years ago contacted him on Facebook and how many times had their photographs— bald, mature, devoid of life, some of them—how many times had those faces borne no resemblance at all to Josh Gardner's or Roderick Forestall's faces as he had known them in high school?

Roderick Forestall and his crowd had not given him the time of day back then. In fact they had made Kerry's life miserable, yet now they were somehow supposed to be his Facebook friends. But this visitor, who wanted to see the antique gate—Kerry had never expected to lay eyes on him again, though hardly a week had gone by in the last three and a half decades when the thought of Xavier Boland had not crossed his mind.

"Keith," Kerry lied. "My name's Keith." He did not feel too bad about the untruth, because he had hated his real name from childhood and had he taken the step of officially changing it, Keith would have been one of his first choices.

*

In 1976 Kerry Fallon had daily wished his mother had not called him Kerry, at least not in Creek Bend. His mother had been innocent: she had been thinking of Irish things, though she was not Irish and had called her other son the normal name of Steve. All Kerry knew was that his name hampered his wish that his grade ten classmates at Dearborn Collegiate High School would stop calling him queer, or a girl. He wished this all the more since he himself suspected he might be at least partly gay. What other explanation could a person have for getting weak in the chest every time Xavier Boland passed by on his way to the only pink locker outside Mr. Stockley's chemistry classroom? How had Xavier got away with it? Xavier had somehow managed to get the painters to leave his locker the old pink shade that had covered all the second-floor lockers prior to the summer of 1975, without Roland Artufi or Kenneth Handler or their friends beating him to a pulp. Maybe you had to be a raging queen for them to leave you alone. Maybe being unsure of what you were was a worse sin in the eyes of the Rolands and Kenneths.

Kerry was sure of some things though. He was sure that he loved, more than anything else in the world, singing harmony. In the Tongues of Flame Pentecostal Assembly everyone knew how to weave in and out of a major chord, and that place felt to him like the home of angels, and he was excited to attend even if his comfort there was tarnished by Pastor Best warning that to be homosexual meant a person was certain to be left behind on the day of the Rapture, and not only that, the person would know a punishment that had no end. But this punishment would wait until Kerry was dead if the Rapture did not come first, and before then, if he were lucky, he would have figured out some way to make peace with god, and with his raging sexual excitement in the proximity of Xavier Boland.

But the Assembly met only three times a week, and only one of those times, Sunday mornings, had an hour given over to choruses, and, he had to admit to himself in all honesty, there were songs he'd far rather sing than *Alive, Alive* or *Let the Anointing Fall on Me.* For his own enjoyment, he had changed some of the words to *I Keep Falling in Love with Him Over and Over Again* so that instead of "Oh what joy between the Lord and I" the chorus spoke of joy with a certain other person, and likewise he altered the words to *I've got a Longing in my Heart for Jesus.* This he did as he walked home from school, making sure no one was close behind, especially not his brother Steve, who specialized in spying on people. But the songs he was really interested in were not these adaptations, nor were they the top ten from CFTO Radio, Your Voice of Reason in the Valley. The songs he loved were songs he had learned from his American cousin Poppy, the summer she had come up from North Carolina to get her illegitimate baby out of her system. The baby had been born by the time Poppy came to stay, born and given away in an adoption process somewhere north of North Carolina but not as north as Creek Bend. He'd been eight and Poppy had to him looked like any normal girl, and he had found it hard to envision her as Clothed in Stain's Disgrace. By the time she arrived at his house, Poppy had forgotten her disgrace enough to begin singing, if she had ever stopped, and she took it for granted that he, Kerry, would be her singing partner on the back steps under his mother's clothesline.

American songs were different. American songs had sunshine in them. They had sunny sides of the street, and riversides, and mockingbirds. They had not only two-part harmony but two-part verses and words, which, overlaid one on another, created a complex lattice that had harmony added to it by-the-way, as if a bird had come to visit and begun singing a third element. There was land in American songs; there were wildwood flowers and bright mornings and sweet little Alice-blue gowns. It was as if everyone in America was getting dressed for a never-ending riverside dance, and sometimes the Americans would sail downriver or fall in love or even murder their lovers and bury them in the reeds, but there was always fresher air than here, and a shining sun, and there were ringlets. Kerry knew in his heart that this was ridiculous and that America was not like that at all, but the songs were joyful and had all these things in them; the songs were a kind of America of their own, and he and Poppy brought it into being with the words and the music and their voices.

"You have a good voice," Poppy said, and he suspected it was true—maybe the songs made his voice even nicer than it was in church, and this was one of the things that sustained him once Poppy had long gone and he was without a singing partner in the world outside church. It sustained him and he saved a dollar a week out of his lunch money and he bought himself a Panasonic cassette tape player, into which he recorded himself singing the melody lines of all the songs Poppy had taught him. When his mother was at Bible study and his dad at the plant and Steve out playing hockey, he played his own voice back to himself and practised harmony with it. He loved this activity, and the longing he had for a friend with whom to sing did not feel quite so painful.

He began to grow his hair a bit longer and to wonder if Xavier Boland might not be so unapproachable after all. Xavier was only one year older than Kerry, and there were friendships that crossed that boundary between grades ten and eleven: Loretta Howell and Gwen Payne, for instance, or Roderick Forestall who had won two peewee curling trophies and the boys on the grade eleven senior team.

There was something of the beauty of America in the way Xavier Boland's locker stood the colour of a wild rose in the otherwise grey-green corridor, and there was something joyful and carefree, like the freedom in American songs, in the very way Xavier Boland moved: not all crunched up and restricted like everyone else, but with his arms loose and long, and his legs too, so they sort of swayed a bit whenever Xavier was on his way somewhere. Kerry began experimenting to see if he too could let his limbs move free and easy like this. At first he did it on his walks home and in the hallway between his bedroom and the kitchen, and then he sneaked a swaying movement or two into his step in the corridor which passed Xavier's locker.

There is energy between people when they have never spoken but have noticed each other's presence, and between Xavier Boland and Kerry this energy existed, but Kerry could not tell its exact meaning. From himself, he knew, came energy that admired, that longed for even a tiny recognition, that felt scared. Now that he had consciously given his own body echoes of the way he believed Xavier Boland walked and moved, this energy of Kerry's felt more exposed and dangerous. He restrained it, but he could not resist lingering whenever he passed the rose locker in case Xavier should come to retrieve his chemistry book or his scientific calculator. And one Thursday Xavier did come—Kerry was on his way to Most Hated of Classes, gym class, when Xavier Boland, alone in the corridor because the bell had rung and they were both late, clicked his combination lock off and reached for a binder off his top shelf.

Kerry suddenly needed to see if Xavier Boland had anything decorating his locker. He might have a music poster, and wouldn't it be amazing if Kerry could know what kind of music Xavier Boland loved the most. He slowed down and looked. Incredibly, there was that sepia Jesus peering soulfully, the one everyone knows even if they are Pentecostal and not given to images of Jesus as much as to flames and doves and bare crosses with light coming off them to show how Jesus is not here any more but has risen to become the firstfruits of all creation. But the Jesus in Xavier's locker had not yet been on the cross. He was praying to his father, his hair long and goldy-brown. He was wearing a pink robe and around him hung ruby-red glass beads, a rosary. Xavier Boland, Kerry realized, was either being sarcastic in his locker decor, or he was a practising Roman Catholic. The only thing Kerry knew about Catholics was that they could get away with anything. They could sin to their hearts' content and then go confess it to the intermediary, the priest. Pentecostals had no intermediary but the Holy Spirit who did not, Kerry's mother said, oppress and terrify the people like Catholic priests did. But still, Kerry knew, before becoming terrified the Catholics could do what they wanted. They could have babies as his cousin Poppy had done and they could parade those babies around in their own homes and even in their church, and all would be forgiven. Even, Kerry felt this flash through him, kissing another boy, loving another boy, instead of a girl … if you were Catholic …

"Are you having a good look?" It was the first time Xavier Boland had spoken to Kerry. His tone was not unkind.

"I was just..."

✦

Xavier Boland lived with his grandmother. She had stucco ceilings with sparkles in them, and her bathroom had a matching pink shag rug and toilet cover and she kept the toilet paper inside a doll with a crocheted skirt. She had a cat and a miniature Hammond organ and over the organ hung her own picture of Jesus holding in his hand his own heart which looked something like a cupcake with wings or flames and a cross sticking out of it. But instead of terror or any other bad feeling connected with priests or churches of any kind including his own, Kerry felt in Xavier's grandmother's house a feeling of the greatest comfort he had ever known. He supposed it was a feeling he had heard and read about but not felt—a feeling of unconditional love. This became more apparent as Kerry observed more and more of Xavier's and his grandmother's life together. Had Kerry's parents caught Kerry with some of the clothes Xavier stored openly in his bedroom, for instance, they would have... what would they have done? Would his father have taken him down to the basement and given him the belt as he had done when Kerry had stolen a *Bounty* bar from Tammy's Convenience when he was eight? Or would they have telephoned Pastor Best and had him come over or sent one of his Youth Leaders over to lay hands on Kerry and cast out demons like they had done to Mildred Stevenson the time Mrs. Tilford and her Ladies' Spirit Association decided that Mildred had the spirit of witchcraft in her? Or would his mother have hidden the clothes from his father—might she have destroyed them and made Kerry promise never to

bring home anything like that again or his father would…
what would his father do? Perhaps living with your grandmother made new things possible. Kerry surveyed the white
bell-bottoms and the other clothes and even purses that Xavier
displayed openly in his room, slung over the chair-back and
hanging out of the drawers. Laid out on the bed was a makeup
case with mascara and eye pencils in it.

"Call me Kay," Mrs. Boland said, but Kerry couldn't even
though she did look like a Kay and she said, "I can't stand being
called Mrs. this and Madam that." His own mother made
home-cooked meals but they were dry pieces separate from
each other on the plate, whereas everything Mrs. Boland cooked
was smothered in gravy, or if it was dessert, in warm custard or
cream or chocolate sauce. Sometimes she made fried chicken
and she didn't put gravy on that but the batter was twice as thick
as the batter on any fried chicken Kerry had ever tasted, and
Mrs. Boland did not formally invite him to supper, she just put
an extra plate out as if Kerry belonged to the family. There was
no accusation of any kind in the air, unlike the atmosphere at
his own house, and he kept fearing that his mother would put
a stop to his visits to the Bolands, but she never did. It almost
made him wonder if his mother was glad to have him out of
the house. The only person at home who said anything about
his new friendship was Steve, who warned if Kerry brought that
fag home here even for five minutes, Steve would personally rip
both their fucken balls off—"and don't think I'm not watching
you and that little fucker's whereabouts."

"I'm not gay," Xavier volunteered to Kerry, who had not
asked. "I just like girls' clothes. My grandmother knows. She
even buys them for me. And I know better than to wear any
of this outside." What seemed outrageous in school—the pink
locker, the way Xavier walked, the length of his bangs—seemed
normal here in his own house. Even the sequined mask with a

feather pluming up from one eye, hung by a bit of elastic over the corner of Xavier's mirror, did not seem out of place.

The singing started as they lay on their backs on Xavier's bed, Kerry's forearm burning from its proximity with Xavier's body but not touching, not ever admitting he would like to touch. There was something about Xavier, now that they had become close friends, that prohibited it. Xavier was exactly like a girl, Kerry realized, only he was a boy. He was like a girl inside a boy's body, and he did not seem to want physical intimacy. Xavier asked the craziest things. He wanted to know if Kerry ever thought about the fact that the moon was moving and so was the sun and all the planets and really, the way days and weeks and years and time happened wasn't like a line of numbers, it wasn't really time at all, it was just things moving around in space and making shadows on each other. Or he wanted to talk about why clothing manufacturers did not make pockets inside your jeans, which would make the jeans smoother and nicer and the pockets wouldn't show under a long shirt and you could keep money a lot safer since no pickpockets could reach it. He talked about how the continents on the world map obviously fitted together like jigsaw puzzle pieces and how come no one ever told them about why that was in geography class, and he knew a lot about fish and aquariums and coral reefs of the world. He liked talking about ideas and Kerry got caught up in it because he would have done anything to lie on that bed close to Xavier, but talking about all Xavier's topics was pretty interesting too. And one day when he felt brave enough he asked Xavier if he liked singing. He was afraid to ask it in case Xavier did not like it, and it might have changed the way Kerry felt about him. He could not admit that he had fallen in love with Xavier, but he was not ready to fall out of love with him either.

"It's okay," Xavier said.

"I love it."

"I know you do. You never shut up singing."

"I don't?"

Xavier laughed. "You don't know you're doing it?"

"Am I doing it loud?"

"No one can pick out the words. You're always mumbling-singing like water in the culvert out back."

"Oh." Kerry was embarrassed.

"Why did you want to know?"

"What?"

"If I like singing."

"It doesn't matter."

"Come on. Why?"

"I like singing … harmonies. I just wondered if you—but you wouldn't."

"I wouldn't what?"

"Sing the melodies. The easy part. You probably wouldn't want to." Kerry was dying to sing duets with a voice not his own tape-recorded voice.

"Are there any easy ones?"

"There's *Down By the Riverside*." They started with that, and by the end of a week Kerry had taught Xavier every song his cousin Poppy had taught him.

"I have to stick a finger in the ear closest to you," Xavier said, "or I'll lose it."

"But then you're too loud."

When they came out for some ham and gravy and mashed potatoes after one particularly successful song session, Mrs. Boland said, "My, that sounded lovely." She had put maraschino cherries on the ham and she had placed the little jar with a few cherries left inside on the table with a tiny spoon in it.

"Did it?" Mrs. Boland was the very first audience Kerry had ever known. He was bursting with pride though he saw Mrs. Boland's comment meant nothing to Xavier, who poured a stream of gravy over his potatoes and started shovelling into them.

"Oh my, yes. I haven't heard anything like that since my husband was alive, when we were young. How do you know all those old songs?"

"Are they old?"

"My dear, they are ancient." And then she started singing a song from memory.

When I grow too old to dream
I'll have you to remember.
When I grow too old to dream
Your love will live in my heart...

She had what they called a voice like a bird, although Kerry knew it was not really like a bird's—it was the voice of a human whose heart was kind. "That song," she said, "was written by Oscar Hammerstein when I was twenty-two."

"Can you teach it to us?"

"I'll play it for you on my organ," she said, and after supper she pulled out her stool and played and sang the song over and over again with Kerry joining in until he had learned it. "I've got some more sheet music in my trunk," she got up, "all Rogers and Hammerstein, and some of the old musicals from Broadway, I used to play them all on my organ." Kerry followed her down the hall and there by her bed that had big cushions all over it she opened a box and took out all kinds of music. Some of it bore pictures or cartoons and Mrs. Boland told Kerry and Xavier they could lie on her cushions with the cat and see if they could sing any of the songs while she made them cocoa. "You'll know some of those songs," she said. "See that one?" She sang *I'm Gonna Wash that Man Right Outta My*

Hair... "You've heard it, I know you have. Everyone's heard that." Mrs. Boland made the cocoa and they drank it on her cushions and she asked them to sing some of their old songs to her and they did, and she fell fast asleep. There was one little lamp on and the cat was asleep too, and soon they were all sleeping in those lovely cushions that smelled of Mrs. Boland's lavender soap.

Long past midnight, just before dawn, Kerry awoke. Someone had turned off the little lamp but he could see the cat, Mrs. Boland, and Xavier, still asleep, in the bit of street-lamp light spilling through the half-open curtains. His first thought was that his mother and father would be angry that he had not come home, but his second thought was more of a sensation than a thought—he realized his body and Xavier's had moved against one another and he had his face against Xavier's chest, and his arm was resting on Xavier's belly and thigh. He reached up with his mouth and barely touched it to the skin of Xavier's face, and at that moment he saw that his friend too was awake. The electric touch of forearm and belly, mouth and face, tantalized them, magnetic and feather-tentative, until Xavier reached Kerry's face and pulled it up to his and kissed him long and hard, his grandmother sleeping on the other side of the cushions. Xavier had always been the braver one, Kerry realized. Xavier the older, Xavier the taller, Xavier the bolder. They took their clothes off furtively and Kerry felt astonished that another human's body felt so hot, like a furnace. It was the most ecstatic event of his life, and the most terrifying. They gave each other the tenderest lovemaking in the world, and it was the first time Kerry had felt anything this exquisite, and he did not care whatever it meant he was. They fell asleep again but it was only five AM when there was a loud knock on the door, then a pounding, and shouting voices.

Mrs. Boland woke, alarmed, and put her dressing gown over her clothes, and let Kerry's father and his brother Steve come in, and two other men who told Mrs. Boland as kindly as they could that she would have to come in to the station on Amherst Road and answer some questions about having a neighbour boy, who was a minor, in her bed, and about sexual practices that had been going on in that bed, practices which Kerry's brother Steve had witnessed through the window and reported to his parents.

After that night it was as if someone had taken Xavier Boland and his grandmother and their house and put them under glass, so that they were no longer part of Creek Bend but more like a forbidden diorama of which no one spoke. Because he was considered a victim, Kerry escaped judgment. He had been lured and had not understood what he was getting into. He was from a good, Bible-believing family for whom many prayers were being waged, as in a war. This was a troublesome blot, an unfortunate disaster, but shame would not spread beyond the doorstep of the Boland house. The Bolands would close their shutters. Mrs. Boland would be placed under probation for three months and her grandson would finish high school in a foster home in another town. The Bolands faded away, though Kerry never forgot Xavier Boland, and now, thirty-seven years later...

*

Kerry tried to go through the motions of showing his visitor the grand old gates that stood behind a bedstead, some plywood and a collection of shovels. Infernally he felt the second verse of Oscar Hammerstein's *When I Grow Too Old to Dream* running through his head: he just could hear Mrs. Boland singing it at her portable Hammond organ:

So kiss me, my sweet
and so let us part
and when I grow too old to dream,
that kiss will live in my heart.

"It's a lovely old gate, for sure," the grown up Xavier Boland said.

"What were you planning on doing with it?"

"I have a client who can use it."

"A client?"

"I find things for people. Big decor projects. Grounds. Windows. Plaster moldings. Gnomes. Statues of horses. You never know what people are going to want. But this gate ... I have a client who's been looking for this kind of gate for a year. How much do you want for it?"

"I don't know how much to ask, to tell you the truth."

"Well my client is going to pay fifteen hundred dollars for that gate. My mark-up is one hundred percent plus the labour of installing it. So how does five hundred sound?"

"Five hundred is exactly what my wife said I'd get for this gate."

"Is your wife always that accurate? Maybe you should send her over to my office. It's hard to find people who are realistic about the price of antiques."

"She's a realistic woman." Kerry thought of all the times Jennifer had been right and he had been wrong about things. About all kinds of things. About money, about the children, about expiry dates on food. He wondered what she might have to say about his story of Xavier Boland, were he ever to breathe a word of it to her.

"Well, Keith," Xavier gave him the money in cash, "I'll bring my truck around from the cul-de-sac and load this up, if you wouldn't mind shifting those few things out of the way while I get Nick and Trevor." He went out and came back ten minutes later with the men, and the gates floated majestically out into the sunlight.

It was only after Xavier had followed them out that Kerry caught himself humming the end of the song that had been playing in his head. He caught himself doing that sometimes, and usually it didn't matter. Usually there was no one around, or the people who were around were used to him doing it. He caught himself humming the end and that made him wonder if he had also, today, in the presence of Xavier Boland, hummed Oscar Hammerstein's song all the way through from its beginning.

Of the Fountain

HE HAD A BROKEN TOOTH and most of his body was stationary, but the feet moved in a special way that I understood. I did not look at him overtly but three men, not a broken tooth among them, they had a good look and I was afraid they'd laugh. We sat near the angel statue under the miniature crabapple trees. It was spring and everyone in Montreal had unfolded. How receptive and joyous we felt about the sun. We gave our bare arms to it for the first time that year. The man with the broken tooth did not appear to be thinking about the warmth on his skin. He was thinking about the accuracy of his feet. He wore headphones and his face was rigid with concentration. It did not seem possible that he should be doing advanced flamenco, not with his too-big sweatpants and, I think, a woman's over-sized sweatshirt, and filthy sneakers. But advanced flamenco it was: I recognized the steps because I had recently given up on flamenco classes myself, having had a merciless instructor. I was sad about it. I'd had high hopes.

"What kind of dancing is that?" asked one of the three men, slim, young and smart. He had a careful five-o'clock shadow. He did not sound mocking and I was relieved. I couldn't have borne it if the smart man had made fun of the dancer.

"Yeah, man ... it looks like some kind of ballroom thing, is it?" said the second one. He too seemed genuine. Maybe they were just nice men. Maybe I was used to toothless, shabbily

59

dressed people being mocked, but maybe they weren't mocked all the time. The dancing man knew they were talking to him but couldn't hear what they were saying because of his music.

He peeled the headphones off. "Pardon?"

Pardon ... He said it so formally.

"You doing some serious footwork there, brother? Some kind of European dance step ... me, I'm into rap."

"Yes, it's ..." and he told them what I already knew.

"Flamenco? That is serious shit, man. More power to you!"

The men watched him for awhile then left, and it was harder for me to observe him unnoticed, but I couldn't help it. He was methodical about his steps. They were correct, but halting. He did not care one little bit what he looked like. If I could have had his attitude while taking my flamenco class I might have made better progress. As it was, I had allowed the teacher to deflate me. One day I came to class wearing a comb that had silk roses attached. I'd bought the comb from a little vintage shop on Avenue Mont-Royal. I wore black and red lace, too. The other students were young, and practised in their street clothes, though of course we all wore proper flamenco shoes studded with nails. The teacher, Juliana de la Fuente, did not wear street clothes. She wore astounding tiered, asymmetrical flamenco costumes, and a different pair of shoes each week: blue, scarlet, silver and gold, with Cuban heels and every other sort of dancing heel. She was a real show-off, is what she was, and when I came in wearing my comb decorated with roses she laughed at it. True, a couple of roses dangled—I meant to stitch them back in place when I found some red or gold thread. She singled me out and mimicked my position—made her arms ungainly and ridiculous—and said I looked *stupid*. I was a bit taken aback—I wouldn't have thought any teacher would do that to a student. Then I wondered if maybe it was because English is her second language.

Maybe she didn't really mean stupid—maybe she meant just that my stance lacked a certain amount of grace, or... never mind. There's no excuse for what she said. It hurt, and I did not go back.

The man with the broken tooth picked his plastic bag off the ground and began to walk away. There was something so humble about him, and about the way he had danced, that I drummed up courage to talk to him. He made me remember what I had wanted out of flamenco in the first place. It had a grandeur to it, a ferocity. An elegance. You could be an old woman and do flamenco. I had seen it. You could be ancient and still do it. It wasn't only for nubile young women. In fact, the older you became, the more you could imbue flamenco with the gravity of your experience. And those nails hitting the floor—they smacked it like horses' hooves, like castanets. The sound was arresting and declarative. You weren't pussyfooting around.

"Excuse me... would you mind if I asked you... I noticed..."

He turned to me politely. He and I were, I surmised, around the same age. We each had a few silver hairs. "Yes?"

"Well I was watching your dancing—I know it's flamenco because I started a beginner's course not far from here, and I... well I wasn't very good at it, and to tell you the truth, the teacher was a bit, well, she was a bit cruel, really... I sort of lost confidence and I was wondering..."

"Was it Juliana?" The broken tooth made him lisp a bit. He was soft around the edges, about twenty pounds overweight. There had been no men in the class I'd taken, no men in any of the classes in that building; not in the corridors nor the stairwells. "It must have been Juliana."

"Juliana de la Fuente. How did you know?"

He had a gentle voice. His hair flew up a bit at the sides. He stood in front of me holding the plastic bag rolled up at the top. It bore a green dollar-store logo. "Believe me," he said, "you shouldn't take anything Juliana says to heart." He looked past the angel and toward the street where the dance school was, between the subway station and a discount jewellery shop. "Did you notice she has a lot of students in her classes? And none of them has taken her class before. She goes through hundreds of students but not very many of them come back to her. That's where I went, at first, but I didn't stay."

"But now you can dance. I was watching. You dance beautifully."

"Thank you. My mother was a dance teacher in Edinburgh. I learned a lot from her. She's eighty-nine now. My name's Ben, by the way."

I told him I had bought a pair of real shoes with the nails, and he said he couldn't afford real ones but had bought a pair of men's Italian shoes with hard soles that clattered.

"I got them for two dollars at the nuns' Thursday bazaar."

I felt bad for having said I possessed real flamenco shoes.

"I find," he said, "you can make do with a lot of improvised things. For instance, a real flamenco hat, for men, is a very expensive black, Spanish hat. It's specialized, and it will be a long time before I can afford one. But today I found a substitute at the dollar-store." He raised the plastic bag. "Would you like to see it?"

"I'd like to see you put it on."

He took out a black straw hat with straight sides and a wide brim and modelled it for me. It transformed him.

"Wow. That's great."

"I'm very pleased. I have to be careful about my spending. Have you ever seen people on the street selling the magazine *L'Itinéraire*?

"I think so ... isn't it a journal of news about street people?"

"Yes. You should, if you have any change at all when these sellers ask you to buy a copy... you should, I don't mean to tell you what to do, but the magazine genuinely helps them to... it helps them transition from being homeless, to having a home. Myself, for instance, I just three months ago, after being homeless for years, got my own apartment because of my job selling the magazine. The next thing I'm saving up for is some plants. I want to grow some plants in pots—I have a little balcony in the back. I'd like to grow edible plants. Lettuces and carrots."

He spoke, I thought, eloquently for a homeless person. He hadn't shaved in a few days but he had that eighty-nine-year-old mother who'd taught him to dance, and he had a desire to grow his own vegetables in pots...

"You don't seem," I ventured, "like a person who has always been homeless, or who has been homeless for most of your life..."

"No," he said. "I had a home. A lot of us had homes. A lot of people who sell the magazine had everything. But something happened that made us lose it all."

He was vague. He implied some sort of story that involved the kinds of things that might make you judge or despise a person. He had done something that had caused other people pain, maybe something worse than pain. It was in the past and there was thick fog between then and now and he didn't want to think about it, though of course it was always there. I put it out of my mind as soon as he said it and focused instead on the Spanish hat and the idea of him tending seedlings in terra cotta pots in the sun on a balcony. This city had balconies for everyone, not just the lucky few. That was one of the reasons I lived here and not in a more utilitarian town.

"The thing I wanted to ask you," I said, "is if you might know another teacher, not Juliana de la Fuente..."

"It means *of the fountain.*"

"What?"

"Her name. You wouldn't think someone with a name as lovely as that would be so uncaring. Fountains are generous... always bestowing."

"Where did you live, before..." It was hard for me to imagine a person who knew the Spanish word for fountain living on the street... a person who used the word *bestowing*.

"Before I got my new apartment?... There are shelters. You get to know where to go. There's the Old Brewery Mission. A lot of men are there quite long-term."

"So, you know another teacher?"

"I have a friend," he took a bashed cellphone out of his pocket and fiddled around to look up a number. "I can call her now and ask her if she minds my giving you her number. She's the real thing. A good flamenco dancer and a caring teacher. I go to church with her and her little girl and she doesn't charge me for lessons." He punched in her number. "Leni?..." He turned away and I heard him say, "... a woman in the park... wondering if... " When he was finished he wrote Leni's number on the back of his dollar-store sales slip and gave it to me.

After that it was a long time before I saw Ben, and when I did he was selling *L'Itinéraire* in front of the liquor store at the outdoor fruit market. I had taken his advice and bought many copies from other sellers by then: a new issue came out every couple of weeks. Sometimes I bought the same issue several times, from different vendors. I bought one from him now and was not sure he remembered me. I had not called his friend Leni or taken any more flamenco classes.

"Ben," I decided to remind him. Normally I'm happy when people forget they know me. I like to go around the fruit market without meeting people to whom I feel obliged to talk, but Ben was reserved, not ebullient. There was no danger he'd try to get too close. "We met in the park and you were practising flamenco. You might not remember ..."

"Right," he said. I still wasn't sure if he had any recollection.

"You gave me Leni's number ... I haven't called her yet ..."

He brightened. "I'm doing a show with Leni next Thursday night."

"You'll be dancing?"

"Yes. It's just a small part."

"Is it open to the public?"

"Of course."

"Could I buy a ticket?"

He told me where to go. I knew the place because it had a cabaret-style set-up and I'd seen a comic book artist do a reading there with a cello player and a burlesque dancer. I didn't want to infringe on Ben's dancing life but if it was a public performance then what was the harm? The tickets were only ten dollars and I bought one. I wanted to see Ben perform his flamenco in a formal theatrical setting—it would bring to the foreground the elegance that came before his fall from grace in the world. I wanted to see that.

But on the night of the show there was a big electrical storm. Traffic chaos filled the whole downtown and crammed bridges leading to the city. The rain slashed down the way it does in New Orleans, like someone is up there chucking celestial buckets down everyone's necks. The subways were down and it was hard to get to the place for eight o'clock, the time printed on the ticket. But I did it. I got there on time and the place was empty. I sat at a little table and drank a gin and tonic slowly, then another, while eleven or twelve more people filtered in. I knew lots of gigs didn't start until a couple of hours after the doors opened, to give people time to warm up and spend lots of money at the bar, but by ten I realized the rain and the traffic congestion had kept everyone away. At ten thirty I spied some glorious Spanish women and men looking tense behind the stage. A woman with a comb full of roses like mine stepped up and explained we were waiting for a busload of ticket-holders stuck on the bridge. Another hour went by and normally I'd have packed it in and gone home to bed, but I couldn't bring myself to leave. At half an hour before midnight five men in black hats took seats onstage, and the women, in full Spanish lace and frill and piled hair and dangling earrings started a real firecracker dance set, all the imploded sexual rage of Spanish womanhood concentrated and then flung into the room with a flare of flaming skirt, a floorboard-shaking hard rain of nails, and those hands, twining incantations in the dim air, rings flashing— their foreheads and arms a sheen of sweat; little puddles glittering in the dips of their beautiful collarbones ... but where was Ben?

The seated men had a special function and he was not among them. They played guitar or clapped: the clapping was fervent and meticulous—it gave voice to the dance and its rhythm was absolute, necessary and serious. The men's role was complicated and mathematical—the rhythm they clapped was far from obvious; completely unpredictable to me, yet perfect and dangerous. I decided Ben was not going to appear onstage after all and resigned myself to watching the show without him. I felt terrible about being one of only a dozen audience members and I'd be damned if I was going to leave before the show was over.

But then began a different kind of song: a break in the feverish Spanish passion wars. One of the men began playing an accordion—*Under Paris Skies*—and the dancer in the white dress—a woman I now supposed must be Leni—floated from stage left to meet ... yes, it was ... in a *beret*, and carrying a folded umbrella ... Ben, floating to take her hand and, straight out of a painting by Toulouse-Lautrec, the two waltzed together while the other dancers caught their breath backstage and perhaps drank gargantuan glasses of cold water. Ben did not do any of the steps I had seen him practise in the park. He was all soft-shoe. Together he and Leni finished the waltz and sailed offstage, not one clack of a castanet. Had he worn a striped jersey with a red cravat? I couldn't remember. I left the barman a tip and rose from my solitary table, which I realized felt lonely, and went home.

What had I expected? A cabaret full of people in mantillas? Bangles to the elbows? Billows of cigar smoke and a few treacherous moustaches? I had not expected a Parisian waltz, that was for sure. How disappointed Ben and Leni and the other dancers must have been, to find not enough people had shown up to make even the appearance of a real audience. How I'd wished I could turn myself into forty people.

I did not see Ben selling his magazines at the fruit market for some time. But when I did, I was with Gerald. I'd told Gerald about Ben, about the day in the park and the flamenco evening and how we should buy *L'Itinéraire* whenever we saw anyone selling it, and he always bought it now. I introduced Gerald to Ben and Gerald bought a copy. It featured a cover story about a New York saxophone player who had been homeless throughout the nineties. Ben and I talked about the show. I told him I'd attended and he said it was too bad about the bridges and the traffic and I agreed, and then Gerald and I went into the indoor part of the market where they sell hard salami studded with lumps of white fat, and where there is sometimes another man, an older man, standing by the garbage can and selling more copies of *L'Itinéraire*. He has a red face and gets out of breath and leans on the garbage can as if it were a podium. Gerald usually buys the magazine from him, and gives him a two-dollar tip each time. So this time, as Gerald approached and the man saw he already held a copy of the magazine, having bought it from Ben, his face grew redder.

"Where did you get that?"

"From Ben," Gerald did not intercept my signal to shut up. "Down there ... outside, in front of the liquor store ..."

The red-faced man is not normally a fast-mover. But he whisked his papers under one arm and leapt away from his garbage can. "He's selling them here, at the market?"

Before Gerald could say anything else, the red-faced man was out of there, round the corner and having it out with Ben over territorial rights. I don't know what happened but I know the next time I saw Ben he had gained another ten pounds and lost about the same amount of life-force. His neck and arms were bruised and he had difficulty coming up with con-versation. He'd fallen off his bicycle, he told me. He'd had a bit of a hard time. A few setbacks. He managed a wan smile. I wondered about his lettuces and carrots in terra cotta pots—whether they'd ever happened, or had remained in the land of dreams. *Come on, Ben*, I wanted to say, *get your trowel, dig the sacred soil.* But who was I to talk, my own flamenco shoes, studded with glorious nails, stuffed in a sack and shoved in a corner of the closet; my comb with its roses collecting dust on top of the Quality Street toffee tin where I keep my needles and thread?

You Seem a Little Bit Sad

SOMEHOW CARA ALWAYS SAW the young man from the halal meat counter after she'd had a mortal blow to happiness. With his slicked hair and his exuberant greeting, he was like some sort of Middle Eastern meat angel, she thought. And how was it that, out of all his customers, who must have numbered in the hundreds each week at that place, he remembered her, later, out of context, as she encountered him by chance on Rue Belanger or on Jean-Talon, on her way for Lebanese cucumbers at the market? And it was not as if she were a good customer of his. Whenever she saw him she felt guilty, as she had bought no more than three packets of meat in her first couple of weeks in the neighbourhood: lamb loin chops, chicken marinated in yogurt and herbs, squares of veal for stew. She had asked him if the veal was pork, to which he replied as kindly as he could that there was no pork in the shop, and though she felt him shower forgiveness upon her for thinking there could be pork at a halal butcher, she felt she had paraded her ignorance before him, and she began going elsewhere for her small pieces of meat. But he saw her on the street nevertheless, and gave her the most enthusiastic greeting, and it was always when she was feeling lonely or blue; when the centre of morose sadness had spilled from that distant location in the farthest sky of her heart and begun saddening the first meadow, the very first ground in her heart's forefront, so that each waking step on the street was a struggle against depression.

At first she misinterpreted his greeting, which seemed sincere and as joyful as an orange bursting with juice, as perhaps a ploy to get her business back again. She fancied he was, if not the sole owner at his butcher shop, at least a co-owner, and her business might mean twenty dollars or even forty a month, and multiply that by however many customers he had, well, it was no wonder he tried to be nice to them. It surprised her that he recognized her even at night, or in a scarf, or with her sunglasses on, or after she had given up meat altogether and lost quite a bit of weight. No matter what she did or how the darkness fell, the halal butcher recognized her on the street and gave her the kind of greeting she might have expected from a beloved old family friend. Perhaps, she thought, he belongs to the Pentecostal church, or to some other evangelical crowd trying with all its might to spread the love of Jesus and gain tithing converts. She did not assume he was insincere, only that it was possible he had been misguided. She did not entertain at all the notion that he might find her attractive, since she had for years considered herself to have grown invisible to men, and besides, he was twenty years younger than she. She decided, unconsciously, not to take his kind greetings personally, yet she could not help feeling precisely the lift of heart one would feel upon being greeted by someone who unreservedly loves us.

What was wrong with summer? Why did spring promise loveliness by way of magnolias and cherry blossoms, only to burn one's retinas and make people sweat from the inside out until they descended into a kind of torpor? And it wasn't just summer and it wasn't just now. It was other times and places—Paris in her youth, for instance. What was wrong with Paris, whose cafés, she remembered, had thrown spears in her heart and given her dreams in which she lost all her teeth? She remembered discovering coriander leaf in a Thai café near Montmartre, and if that wasn't the very taste of springtime turning into a lonely, deep summer heat, then Cara did not know what was. Even now that she had a husband

and a child and a clothesline that crisscrossed clotheslines of some European neighbours who handed olive bread and arancini over the garden fence, the lonely taste of coriander made her suffer, as did the clanging of Montreal's church bells and the sound of the postman dropping her bills and her husband's *Harper's Magazine* through the letter slot onto the doormat, now that their dog had died. Foolish, barking, hair-shedding nuisance of a dog—fifteen-year-old hound of stinkiness—when he had been alive she had not realized that she loved him. Now, with the days topping thirty degrees, she had to wear her sunglasses or the neighbours would see she had been sobbing, again, about the dog's death. How could you not realize you loved something or someone for fifteen years? What was wrong with her? Before she had moved to Montreal, a shop girl in her tiny town had once bought her a coffee in a paper cup at the gas station. The girl had been no more than twenty, and had simply paid for one of the gas station's coffees and given it to Cara. Had Cara, even then, broadcast to the entire world that she suffered from a terrible loneliness so deep it made her at times unable to function? Did the halal butcher boy see this now, as he approached her, two weeks after her dog had died? She had not seen him in short sleeves before and had not known his arms were covered in thrilling tattoos. He had a life outside the butcher shop, of course, but she had not thought about what it might entail. Were there not Irish songs about butcher boys? She believed there were. She had, in fact, once had a crush on a boy who would later become a butcher. There was a letter from him in a box somewhere, written after he had begun his apprenticeship. In it, he had been stung by a bee, and this was the cause of a delay in his training. There had been no word of romance in his letter, or in anything about him—but it had been understood that something might happen between them if she were to come back to the town where he lived, the town where they had met when she visited for one summer. And what of this butcher boy, here in Montreal, twenty years her junior, now that she was middle aged? Was there a hint of romance there? She had told herself there was not, but…

It was insane to invoke her mother, but the mind knows no rules about what it will or will not throw on the shores of one's consciousness, and now Cara remembered everything her mother had said about tattoos. It was impossible for Cara to simply observe this young butcher's tattoos without hearing her mother beseeching her never to get a tattoo herself, since the human body was meant to continue unmarked, just as it was from birth. How would it be to gaze upon this man's tattoos and truly see them, and appreciate them for their artwork and their stories, without a layer of her mother's disapproval interfering in the act of observation? It was impossible, for the reason of the tattoos alone, let alone the age difference, the fact that Cara had a husband she loved, or any other factor… impossible to entertain romantic thoughts about the middle eastern butcher. Still, she entertained them. They were not fully formed thoughts, not complete at all, but they existed as he walked toward her on this day in which she still felt heartbroken over the loss of that nuisance of a dog. She saw him getting ready to give her his enthusiastic greeting, and she decided she would be the first to speak this time. She forgot they had always spoken French to each other.

"Hi, how are you doing?"

"Pretty good." She remembered the French now, and was surprised that he spoke English perfectly well. The baker and the café owner and all the proprietors in her neighbourhood spoke French to her although French was not their native language, except for the Haitian grocer. They were Italian and Japanese and Lebanese, and she enjoyed the idea that these people for whom French was a second language, as it was for her, had taught her the words for many kinds of foods and had also been responsible for her learning a fair amount of French syntax. But now the butcher said, "Yes, pretty good, because I have quit my job and am going back to Mexico to get my wife. She is coming with me then, and we are going to New York."

He was Mexican! He was not Middle Eastern at all, and never had been. Why had no one in Cara's school days ever taught her the slightest bit of proper geography? Why, even now, in middle age, could she not tell the difference between a Mexican butcher and a Middle Eastern one? He ate pork all the time when he was not at work, and when he was at work he was not the co-owner at all, but an employee.

"It was," he told her now, "a hard place to work."

"I'm happy for you that you will be with your wife." It was true, Cara was happy for him. She was happy for him because he had welcomed her when she had been a newcomer to town, not knowing her from Adam yet treating her with his enthusiastic smile.

"We have been apart for a year and a half."

Cara wondered if he had had girlfriends. She wondered anew if she herself might have been considered by him as a prospect, despite her age. She found it hard to imagine a man going without a lover for a year and a half. Was it her imagination, or did trouble ripple across his face as he thought of how it would be to get used to being together again with his wife, after all this time? It would be hard for anyone. It would be hard, in some ways, for his wife, too. Maybe there were many things he did at home that got on her nerves, that she had not had to put up with for all this time. Would they have a happy reunion?

"In New York," he said, "I will be able to dance more salsa than I can here. Salsa is everywhere there." He looked happier about this than he had looked about his wife. Cara imagined him gliding across every last part of a vast dance floor with his smile and his tattoos. He was becoming more interesting by the moment, and she did not even know his name. They were talking with each other now like two very good old friends. Lilac time had nearly passed and now there were extravagant irises bursting open in all the gardens behind the wrought iron railings.

Salsa frightened Cara, as did hot springs, fondue parties and the double-cheeked kiss of greeting practised by everyone in Montreal. She did not like anything that prevented her from exercising her natural reserve, or that might involve an accidental exchange of sweat or saliva, and this whole interchange with the now Mexican butcher had always threatened to become overly demonstrative in some way, yet she had been the first to say hello this time. It would take only a slight departure and she might find herself following this man home to his bachelor's apartment where he might make that delicious spicy soup she had tasted in the Mexican café down the street, the soup containing hominy and a chunk of perfectly roasted pork. Perhaps his pillow would be visible through his bedroom door, a dent from his head still there from this morning. She was, in fact, a person who required the open end of a pillowcase to face away from her so that she never saw it, so that all she saw of even her own pillow was an unbroken puff of plain smoothness. This conversation was, really, quite frightening the more deeply she entered it. She felt certain she was about to be invited to the last salsa evening the Mexican butcher might know here in Montreal before the arrival of his wife, and she did not have the faintest idea how to dance. Dancing alone was different—she had always danced alone and would be the first to get up at any dance that did not require one to be part of a couple. In fact, strangers had asked her if she were not a professional dancer or a dance teacher, when they saw her dance alone. But dancing with a partner was different. She could not bear it when a dance partner took her hand and did that horrible thing whereby they lift one's arm and proceed to duck under it and twirl around and begin fishing around with their other arm to link up in some sort of mysterious order of motion that surely no one could be expected to follow. Life was full of things like this, and she avoided them at all cost, which was probably why, she now saw, she felt so unhappy and alone so often. The whole world was not afraid of dancing together as she was. The whole world knew, she saw all of a sudden, how to take the hand of a Mexican butcher and twirl with him and dance as dancers had done from the beginning of dance itself, which was the beginning of humanity, a club to which Cara had never felt she belonged. Why did it take, for her, such special bravado to dance, to laugh, to twirl, to speak to a stranger on the avenue? Why was it that others knew what life was all about while she did not even know how to make small-talk at the most casual gathering? Who was the Mexican butcher's wife, and how was it that Cara knew the wife was a real human being whereas she, Cara, was…

"You seem a little bit sad," the Mexican butcher said.

Quickly she fumbled around in her mind for a reason, because you couldn't blame coriander you had eaten in Paris decades ago, nor hot springs that had frightened you in New Mexico, nor the fact that you wished you could dance salsa like an expert, nor the fact that summer had arrived with a strange, searing baldness about the sun that blinded and scared you and made you stricken with loneliness, and she said, "Yes, it's because I lost my dog. My dog died."

"The lovely black dog—I remember seeing you with that dog. I am sorry your dog died."

And he was. The lovely Mexican butcher was sorry Cara had lost her dog. He would understand, had she told him, just how it felt when the postman dropped her bills and magazines on the hall carpet with a thump and there was no corresponding howl. He would know just what she meant if she told him she couldn't imagine the dog unable to hear that sound he had always howled at maniacally, with an earth-shattering yowl that always woke the baby in the upstairs apartment.

"I imagine my dog," she told him now, "somewhere too far away to hear it when the mailman drops a letter through our door. I can't see any other reason why the dog doesn't still howl. In fact I imagine if I listen carefully enough, very very carefully, I will hear him howling from wherever it is he has gone. Isn't that silly?" This was a thing Cara had not even told her husband. It made her feel ridiculous but now she was glad someone knew. Someone knew her dog had not died but had merely moved far away to a place where she could no longer find him. She knew, somehow, that the Mexican butcher, with his wife who had been gone a year and a half, with the salsa lessons to which he looked forward in New York, with his own pork consumption at home after work, when he had still had his job, and with the little cloud that had rippled across his face while he thought of how things would be different soon, when he was no longer single and would need to consider the happiness of a wife who was present rather than distant… yes, this man would understand how the distance of her dog made her sad. He would even understand that there was a lot more to her melancholy than the dog itself, although he might not ask her to go into detail. Sometimes, with the right person, you did not have to map out every coordinate of a situation. Some people were naturally sympathetic, and the Mexican butcher was like that.

"I wish you," she said, making a little prayer-fold with her hands against her heart, a thing she sometimes liked seeing people do but which she never did, "the happiest life in New York." It was the first time she felt that the blessing had gone from herself to the Mexican butcher. Usually it was the other way around.

"Thank you," he said, and they parted, for the last time, on the street that would miss him when he was gone, since that particular street, though it saw magnolia and cherry blossom and iris and soon roses as well, did not see many men with the Mexican butcher's excess reserves of kindness.

The Zamboni Mechanic's Blood

My husband came home from his new job at the funeral service and made miso soup while I checked the mirror to see if those were really moustache hairs I'd noticed on my own face, glowing in the sun. Had he noticed the hairs?

"No."

"Please tell me honestly."

"I've known a lot of women with moustaches." He chopped leeks. He had thrown his fedora with the red feather in it on our water cooler. He wasn't sure if he liked the new job. He looked good in that fedora but he was putting a dead man in the ground every day.

"Have you?"

I wondered about the moustachioed women my husband had known. I saw them in my mind. Moustaches and long hair. Moustaches and hot pink patent leather handbags. He had never mentioned these women before.

"We were talking in the church, me and one of the other porteurs. He used to be a Zamboni mechanic for all the big NHL games at the old forum. It was great. He only had to work three hours and they gave him a nice ticket up close."

"Does this fall into the category of other part-time jobs more desirable than the one you just found at the funeral service?"

"Eh?"

"The Zamboni mechanic."

"It was great for him—he saw all the games ..."

"Wait. We were just talking about moustaches."

"I mean he had a moustache. A nice little grey moustache, nice and full and wide, from the nose to the lip. And it stopped at the edge of the mouth, on a 45. He'd sit with the wives of the hockey players."

"He told you this today?"

"Yes, it was a Ukrainian funeral. The priest had red robes all embroidered: a beautiful young man. We had to place four chandeliers around the body."

"With burning candles?"

"Yes and the songs were lovely. Different from any other kind of song. And I saw another thing: a young man crying, and an old man wiping away his tears."

"And the Zamboni mechanic was telling you about his job."

"Yes, in the lobby, before the graveyard. One time he got called all the way up to Quebec City to fix a Zamboni that had stopped in mid game. Big fines for that. No one would admit it ran out of gas. Pranksters are always doing that to the fork-lift guys in warehouses as well. Zambonis and forklifts run on propane. All you have to do is open the valve. And one time Patrick Roy got knocked out."

"Patrick Roy?"

"He's the most decorated goalie in the NHL. He got knocked out and his wife was sitting beside the Zamboni mechanic and she grabbed him and ripped his shirt and dug her long fingernails in his arm and drew blood. He had to throw away that shirt."

Leek and carrot shavings floated in the miso. We'd eat then walk to the market for café au lait at the place we call the garage door. That was one thing about his new job. After a three-hour funeral he could do what he wanted, but I knew he didn't like it. All the porteurs were a bit older than he was. They were semi-retired. The Zamboni mechanic had told him he regretted deciding to become old too fast. Sometimes a widow flung herself on a coffin and the porteurs had to be careful not to drop it. You were the porteur of other people's passion, and if you weren't careful you missed the moment when a red-feathered bird stole off with your own.

ANHINGA

SANIBEL ISLAND FELT SOMEHOW Victorian to Claire, or it felt, at least, like something that belonged to a Victorian concept of exotic lands. She couldn't stop wondering how Darwin might have felt when, as a young man, much younger than she was now, he sailed for the first time to a place like this and saw with his own eyes how plants and animals had adapted to tropical conditions. Here on Sanibel the anhingas and other dinosaur-like birds were sheathed in platelets of armour against wind and heat. Their size was unnerving. The vegetation, too, was armoured, palm trees and prickly pears bristling with shingles and blades, paddles and spines. Despite all this protection, strangler figs managed to twine around exposed trunks with ever-constricting tendons, gradually throttling the life out of them. Glittering lizards forever darted from under the varnished bush outside her rented cottage, startling her; miniature versions of the malevolent iguana her daughter had volunteered to have in the house one summer because the science teacher's wife was terrified of it. Even the local people looked reptilian. She'd wanted heat and respite from a Montreal winter, but this was comfortless. It wasn't really hot enough—she should have gone farther south—a raw wind thrashed leaf-plates and scaled pinions until they threatened to fly off their outlandish owners and slice into her temples, leaving her sprawled and bleeding on the bike path.

What was it one of the Victorian poets had written, mourning an absence of things diminutive and northern, about a gaudy melon flower? One of the Roberts... Stevenson? No, it was Browning... yes, Browning, three years younger than Darwin, homesick on his own exotic travels. *Home-Thoughts, from Abroad.* That was the poem. Well, there was nothing diminutive here, the airport road lined with synthetic stucco buildings stretching for miles and decorated with molded urethane medallions, painted foam balustrades and non-supporting Tuscan, Corinthian and Doric columns: conglomerate commercial bungalows whose faux stone arches bore fibreglass signs advertising ribs and burgers along with the most involved bodily restructuring: Corneal Transplants, Kidney Extraction, Neck Lifts and Fat Transfer... all of it as ghastly as she'd imagined Florida might be... what had possessed her to come? *Imagine a Stunning New You*, the signs proclaimed. *Begin Your New Life Today!*

Sanibel Island was different, it was true: it had a great deal of wilderness preserved by benevolent citizens and the government. On trees that fringed the little beach that her cottage brochure had promised—not the big beaches everyone visited, but a scrap of sand hardly existent at high tide—the ospreys were nesting, and they glared at her as if they would peck her eyes out if she made one wrong move. And the pelicans—how ungainly they were, plunging for fish with a great splash as if someone had lobbed them into the water and they had no control over their own tangle of wing and claw.

Her cottage was next to a famous little café that had a long porch and many kinds of ice cream that you could not persuade the staff to administer in anything but triple mounds no matter how you beseeched them to give you one small scoop on a child's cone. She tried not to lose her temper but lost it anyway, as she had done at home over trivial matters with her loved ones … when the pretty student handed her the teetering scoops she tore off the top two, threw them in the bin and grabbed a napkin for the impossible task of cleaning the stickiness. Way to go, Claire—you're really going to enjoy that ice cream now.

The porch was lined with painted recliners, filled with ancient couples from Michigan and Illinois, couples who'd stuck it out with each other through intense underground hostilities and now shared expressions of fathomless grumpiness that no amount of Sanibel Coconut Banana Tango could help. Morbidly obese, legs spindly, they'd come in cars, cars, cars that choked Periwinkle Way, driving the locals crazy with the schizophrenic knowledge that without tourists this place would be a forgotten backwater, but with them … god, what was it?

On the big beach a bike ride away, near the lighthouse and pier, Claire watched them walk barefoot on the cold sand, picking up moon shells and clamshells and lightning whelk egg cases that they all mistook for eel skeletons: discs of cartilage on a spiralling cord. A net bag of shells in one hand, cellphone in the other …

"Did Joan feed the rabbit?… Has Moe moved Aunt Cindy's car? Don't forget to shovel her back gate … "

In the fish shack on Periwinkle Way a woman in capris exhibited the family's latest photos on her phone, the friend dutiful … "Oh my, nice, yes, I love your new yellow countertop."

In the restaurants it was impossible to get a meal that would have passed muster had anyone involved in its preparation performed the most rudimentary taste test. Arugula salad with buffalo mozzarella and heirloom tomatoes sat drenched in vinegar. The butterfish, from which, it was true, the waiter had tried to dissuade her, had the texture of a candle extinguished just as the wax had turned soft throughout. Everything here was meant for tourists, for sale, and not for real life, which was why Claire congratulated herself on the fact that she had at least rented a cottage that had a two-burner stove, which meant she could cook rice and beans and a bit of kale, or boil the tiny non-stick pot for tea, though she could hear her mother now telling her how non-stick coatings break off and *migrate* into one's body taking up permanent residence, being made of elements the body can't recognize as substances to be eliminated. They migrated, undetectable, to the far reaches of every capillary.

Claire had realized, too late to do anything about it, that the people she had not brought to Sanibel with her were nevertheless in her thoughts, and that she was in for a fortnight of torturous loneliness. Nobody was here to share the absurdities or the hot sun or the rather frightening birds and plants, yet she would know exactly how they'd have reacted to everything here and what they would have thought of it all. She would have their commentary—imagined, yes ... but startlingly realistic in her mind—without any warm-bloodedness or laughter she might have shared had she had the sense to bring any of them along in person.

She'd gotten the wrong impression about the locals from the taxi driver who'd driven her at night from the airport. He was from Kentucky and had moved here to look after his parents. His mother could no longer cook or remember anything and his father had both hips replaced but it wasn't going well ... yet in spite of this the taxi driver, Callum Tyree, possessed an air of real easygoing friendliness, even happiness. He was happy this fare was taking him over the causeway from Fort Myers to Sanibel.

"When I've dropped you off," he said, "I'm not gonna go back to work right away. I'm gonna take a ride around the island. You're gonna love it there… just watch out for the alligators."

"… really?"

"I believe," he said slowly, "a lady got eaten last year by an alligator on Sanibel. Didn't get away fast enough."

"Are alligators fast?"

"They can sprint. Probably she had something wrong with her, that lady. Probably she couldn't get up and run all that fast, for some reason." He fell into silence and she noticed he was not an aggressive driver. He let other drivers cut in front of him and he hung back until the way was easy again. "I found a boat on Craigslist for two thousand five hundred… thinking of buying it and living on it."

"I always loved houseboats."

"Got a buddy moored off Sanibel with the shrimp boats— doesn't even have sails. Boat's just an old wreck—when he wants something in town he goes ashore in a rowboat. You can live almost for free if you got a boat like him."

"A person can still do that?"

"Sure."

"Mmm… I wouldn't mind… bobbing on the water, being rocked to sleep… you can stay out there for free?"

"If you want you can pay a hundred and fifty dollars for a mooring and that'll get you electricity and a shower…"

They stopped at a convenience store so she could buy breakfast things for the cottage in the morning. He came in with her and bought a bag of chips and stood munching them while she found apples and eggs. The store did not have an onion in it. They met at the last aisle in front of a display of straw hats.

"This one here," he picked up a dramatic number furled at the sides, "is a real Kentucky hat."

"I'd like to see you put it on."

He sported it for her.

"Looks pretty good."

They'd gone on like that for the rest of the ride, and when he pulled up outside the pitch black cottage area—there were no streetlights so as not to disorient migrating birds—he got out of the car to make sure she found her key and got in all right. It was one of those vacation rentals where the owners are offsite. Her bike was waiting for her under a tree that had orange flowers all over it. The cottage was simple as she'd hoped, advertised as an old-style Florida beach cottage. The interior walls were pale blue—there was a writing desk, a bed, a two-burner stove and a little kitchen table and fridge. Because it was a bit like the kind of simple living arrangement she imagined his friend had on the boat with no sails, she asked Callum Tyree as he hovered near the taxi if he'd like to look in at it.

"I'd suggest," he said, "putting your bike inside for the night, or it might get stolen." He stepped in and stood for a second near the wicker couch then stepped out again, but for the moment that he was inside she felt the loneliness of the night and the slight impropriety of having asked him to come in and look—would he… ? No, he would not take it the wrong way, and she was a big woman, used to unconsciously assessing her ability to fend off physical attacks or advances… it was in her imagination, any hesitation on his part to leave—he left with perfect politeness, but the friendly good humour of their talk… had it almost been a kind of planning, together, of a possible life out there on the water in an old houseboat among the shrimp fishers? No, she told herself, it had not been that at all. But it had been fun—she hadn't known then that trying on the hat and discussing the vagabond life would be the only real human conversation she'd enjoy the whole time she was on Sanibel. From the time Callum Tyree left her alone in the cottage, she would be utterly and essentially lonely. What a fool, coming by herself. She was a woman who did not know the first thing about her own temperament. Solitude? Why in the name of all that was alive on this earth—anhingas, orange flowers, shrimp fishermen—why had she imagined solitude was a thing she wanted?

By her fourth day she had ridden all the bike paths and seen all she could bear of geriatric beachcomber couples tolerating each other in cold fury. Even the little beach where she could sit alone with the ospreys felt full of malevolence—she couldn't blame the ospreys, on whose nesting grounds intruders continually encroached, but she did not want her eyes plucked out. There was an outfitting company that worked with the big wildlife reserve toward the northeastern part of the island, and you could rent a canoe and go around the mangroves, where there would be herons and brown pelicans and oyster beds and… she had not quite figured out the alligator situation—it was something she could ask the outfitters. The ospreys, menacing in their own way, had taken days to disturb her completely, whereas the tourists had done so in far less time. Maybe the herons and alligators or whatever lived in the mangroves… maybe they wouldn't be so… The people she had left at home made their views known. The eldest daughter urged her to go deeply into the mangroves, to the most dangerous place possible. The youngest said, *Don't get et.* Her mother shuddered in revulsion.

The canoes were blue and made of scratched plastic. They looked like toys. It seemed unlikely that any outfitter would provide such canoes if there were real dangers out there. It would be like floating around in an elongated Frisbee. She had slid down the hill in Montreal's Parc du Mont-Royal on a dollar-store toboggan more substantial than those canoes.

"I noticed," she told the person upstairs in the gift shop as she handed over her credit card, "on my bike, on one of the bridges... a sign that said do not feed the alligators, and I wondered..."

"Hmm..." thinly veiled scorn.

"I mean I understand why no one should feed them—what I'm wondering about is, exactly how it works... I mean..."

"Just look where you're going. For one thing, you're probably not going to get that close to one, but if you see one lying across the path..."

"Okay."

"And an alligator is not likely to consider you as food because you're—for one thing—huge..."

"What do alligators normally consider food?"

No wonder the woman was looking at her that way. Why, Claire wondered, had seventeen years of formal education not implanted an image somewhere in her brain of an alligator eating something... She suddenly remembered that her brother Craig had camped in Orlando in his van for a year and had mentioned to her that he tossed the alligators strawberry shortcake and hard-boiled eggs. Possibly this image had supplanted others she'd learned from her high school geography teacher, Mr. Ollerhead. Such names her teachers had possessed... there had been a Mr. Wigglesworth too, a fact her daughters refused to believe.

"Birds. Frogs. Raccoons. Fish. Turtles. Snakes."

"Okay, so... under normal circumstances..."

"Sometimes a deer or a cow, depending..." She handed Claire the Visa receipt to sign, and told her to be down at the water's edge in fifteen minutes where Chris would give her a canoe.

Down on the beach the water looked flatter, and all the people paddling happily—in pairs, she noticed—appeared to her like children on paddleboats in an English park, as if there were no manatees or alligators in the water at all. Manatees, she remembered reading in the magazine in the seat-pocket on the plane, were the closest relative of the elephant: she had no idea how large they grew, but as Chris pushed her offshore with one hefty shove, she imagined many of them must be at least as big as her canoe, and if they chose to put their heads up while underneath her ... she had read, too, that the bay was shallow, but even so ...

She decided to head for mangroves in the mid distance, in an area where she could see no other canoes. It took her a good half hour—the boats were unwieldy compared to real canoes in which she'd traversed lakes in Newfoundland and Quebec—and once she approached the mangroves she realized she'd left behind the hum and drone of sound—human sound—that had formed subliminal background noise on Sanibel. Each drip from her paddle-ends amplified, as did the cheeps and hoots and rustlings in the tangle of mangrove leaves and roots. She examined the roots, remembering a booklet in the gift shop that had explained their network of gnarls and caverns were little houses—nurseries—for three quarters, was it? ... of the fish and bird and alligator life on Sanibel and the mainland. Three quarters! The darkness was asquirm, and here she was, alone ... What would happen if she were to land her canoe on the roots and investigate them? With her paddle she prodded and found they moved slightly but did not give way. Had other people got out of their canoes and taken private journeys into what the guide-books called walking trees?

In Canada she would have been made to wear her life jacket, but here, they'd told her she could use it as a cushion—only children under eleven were obliged to wear them—so she had not put it on and she saw no reason why she might need it while walking in the trees unless ... what had Callum Tyree told her? "Just don't go walking in the woods ..."

But were mangroves the same as woods? Weren't woods more like the palms and swamp ash trees and subtropic bushes in the island's interior? Mangroves were animate … if you licked them the leaves were salty because they drank estuary water and shed the salt—some leaves turned yellow—here there were lots—and fell in the roots, decomposed and became part of the mucky, nourishing mud-bed that the trees again consumed … sacrificial leaves, she'd heard someone say. She liked the efficiency of this, and the fact that some leaves and not others were sacrificed, though all were borne on the same kind of wood.

Not a good idea, announced her brother Craig, whom she had not seen in five years, as she stepped out of the canoe and tested the mat of roots with her foot. Her younger daughter agreed with him from afar. The elder one lifted an eyebrow. Her mother had put on her lavender-filled eye mask. The only person in her acquaintance who was the slightest bit encouraging was Callum Tyree, who stuck his hand in his chip bag and, under that Kentucky hat, amiably offered, *You should be all right, long as you tie up that loose sneaker-lace.*

Nobody said anything at the outfitting headquarters about not getting out of the canoe, said Claire.

No, said her mother, and in that one word lay a world of remonstrance.

Why are you doing that, pet? asked her dad, the most understanding of all—he was a man whom she could imagine venturing deep into the mangroves with a scientific curiosity—yes, curiosity propelled her, too, although part of the attraction was that she had an idea animals might be willing to let her stay here with them, as long as she showed quietness and respect. They might—she realized this was hardly sensible, yet—they might somehow enfold her …

She was aware that this was terrain liable to behave in ways unknown to her, yet she walked a few metres, hanging onto overhanging branches and testing, ever so carefully, each foot-fall. She looked for eyeballs in the dark tangle. Of course there were no eyeballs. She'd done this at home—walked into wilder-ness hoping for acceptance, for some sort of magic whereby she and the non-human life would extend to each other a kind of miraculous communication. Wasn't that what everyone wanted from a trip into wild parts of the world? But wildlife did not come forward. She checked the tangle of roots for code, as if it held a calligraphy waiting to be deciphered.

Stay in one place, quietly and for a long time, she recited, and you'll learn something. She wouldn't mind staying here half a day, waiting motionless… but that was a lie. Twenty minutes was pushing it—she fidgeted and twitched. Here, in the nursery of the ocean, life teemed, protected and hidden. She was looking too hard, downward, upward to where the salty leaf-tangle rose speckled with pieces of sky. She shortened her depth of field and tried to relax as if it didn't matter what she missed, and began to see spiders the size of walnuts scut-tling on the mangrove trunks, then—with a spoked, vampiric shawl drawn about its neck—an anhinga, ten feet over her head, motionless, having sat there the whole time.

The anhinga waited for something. All life, Claire realized, was waiting, and the thing that made the difference between human happiness and the kind of sanity-ransacking loneliness she now felt in this armoured wilderness, was that you either did it alone, or you were sensible and you waited with other people, and while you all waited, you bought bottles of wine and some good bread and maybe a couple of hard salamis mar-bled with fat, and you enjoyed yourselves. You put on some music, for god's sake, and you danced.

There was a particular drama she'd learned about among the pamphlets in her cottage. Anhingas fastened their nests on branches overhanging alligator waters. If a predator approached the nest, the branch bent and the predator slid into waiting jaws. Which meant that yards from where Claire stood in the mangrove roots, there would lurk expectant gators, and she had brought neither strawberry shortcake nor boiled eggs.

Her canoe, she saw through the bushes, now bobbed up and down—had the tide risen? She feared it might break free from the mangroves and… she'd better get a move on. Had it already…

The ground was not ground but a collection of intertwined, upside-down limbs. Her glasses slipped and as she lunged for them she felt her heel and ankle and knee cram into a space… her left leg was down there, really down there in the roots, and her glasses… she knew exactly which opening they'd fallen through, and she reached, yet could not feel her glasses: without them she wasn't blind, exactly, but—and they had cost— those bloody glasses were unbelievably expensive.

She knew she'd be able to get her leg out of the mangrove roots if she remained calm and, by degrees, adjusted the awkward way her body now connected with… you couldn't call it land, or ground… with terra infirma… terra incognito, terra that was pretty terrifying if you thought about it too carefully, and she hadn't been—there was no doubt about it—she knew what they'd say; her mother, her daughters—she hadn't been careful enough. She'd been far from careful, in fact. She bit her bottom lip and tried to mark the place where her glasses had descended—if only she had a bit of red wool and could reach to tie a bow around that root—she knew she'd lose the place once she took her eyes off it. The roots were all the same.

The leg had jammed into a deep fork and her arms did not possess strength equal to the task of… it was absurd. She calmly noticed a stretch of water visible beyond her canoe. If another paddler were to enter that stretch she could shout. If nobody came, if she stayed quiet and felt her body carefully, she'd be able to manoeuvre the leg, unscrew it from the crooked track into which it had forced itself. She noticed the stuck foot, deep down, had begun to feel damp.

Was it her imagination, or had the roots wound themselves more tightly around the leg? Woman Eaten by Mangroves, she read in next week's edition of *The Montreal Gazette*. Head Found Atop Roots. Body Partially Digested by Mud Underlay. Missing Foot Supposed Eaten by Alligators. Passport and Credit Cards Undisturbed in Wallet. She watched the wretched canoe float slightly farther away. Why had she not thought to tie it to the mangroves using her handy dandy all-purpose scarf, instead of leaving that garment like a puff of collapsed magnolias near her life jacket?

Chris would be watching for her, she reasoned. He'd expect her to return at her appointed time. There'd be a half hour's grace period, then maybe an hour of looking for her in real canoes that they surely kept in a bunkhouse somewhere, equipped with lifebuoys and canisters of emergency drinking water. They'd spot her canoe… was that its stupid blue nose bobbing behind a distant oyster bed? They'd circle this island in no time, calling out the name on her credit card, and she'd reply as nonchalantly as a person could, that she was here, she'd fallen and… then they would come and get her. They'd have some sort of slim but powerful saw blade to get these roots off her leg.

The anhinga had not moved. Why didn't the bird do something? Was it sleeping? Poised, its wings were both gathered and fanned, as if awaiting some signal to expand them in an extravagant sweep that would change all things. She waited a long time without panicking, but realized two things had happened which she had not counted on. Her canoe had vanished—who knew how far it had drifted? And the light, which in her earlier confidence she had supposed might outlast her predicament, had begun to fail. Was it possible sundown could come before Chris and his colleagues found her? Would they have to use bullhorns and flares?

She focused on the anhinga, which remained still until she could not differentiate between its outline and the shadows around it. Scraps of sky among the leaves turned red, then an alarming shade of mauve. In her wallet Claire remembered she'd stuffed the taxi receipt Callum Tyree had given her. It had his signature on it, his taxi number and the name and telephone number of the company for which he drove cars. She pictured herself carefully affixing the card to the anhinga's leg and instructing it to find Callum Tyree who would understand where it had come from. Find Callum Tyree and get him over here before night, she whispered at the bird, and as she whispered she remembered from some part of her past having learned—had it been from Mr. Ollerhead or Mr. Wigglesworth?—that alligators are nocturnal. She remembered how on Sanibel there were no streetlights so as not to disturb the life that now surrounded her. She'd thought it charming her first three nights here, and had made sure to cycle down the bike paths to her cottage by sunset every evening. She'd lounged on the bed from eight til midnight eating boysenberry yogurt and switching between local news channels: Charlotte County Couple Burned to Ashes in Smokeless House Fire, and *Stripper Confidential*: "I'ma gonna tell you right now, Mikhaila, if mah man ever tole me I hadda axe him permission before I goes out an' earns the money I needs tah feed mah chile ..."

She'd suspected the mangroves were drawing her deeper into themselves, and had measured the position of her navel against a certain horizontal root. Now that root was a thumb-width higher than her navel. Or was it a different root? How was it possible that neither Chris, nor any colleague of his, had yet appeared? She'd long suspected that most people who worked for somebody else didn't care about the details of their jobs. There was a relaxed, holiday-camp atmosphere at the outfitting shop, not the vigilance one might expect. Workers had a hardened attitude—but who wouldn't, on an island overrun with strangers who came for no other reason than to get away from the northern freeze, rubbing up against this warm body of land with a kind of desperate, heat-seeking friction.

That's what I've done, too, Claire thought. But I lack an instinct that makes other users grab what they want and escape. I'm not a person who gets away with things. I pretend to care, pretend to be curious, to want to get to know the warm body—but it knows. The land knows all I care about is the *heat*—I'm greedy for it...

There was a horrible grating sound and a scream, then a flapping like a tent in the wind and a huge splash—then silence. The anhinga was gone and she was alone. Yet a notion persisted that the anhinga knew her exact location. It had her coordinates. It would get to the mainland when she could not. Maybe it was on its way there now. If only it could communicate her plight to Callum Tyree or to his unnamed friend living in the houseboat without sails among the shrimp fishermen, she might get to step onto that houseboat—mauve and floating in the dusk—paper lanterns strung all around, waiting to be lit.

Madame Poirer's Dog

When Doctor Gisele came this morning to assess me again, she asked me to name an animal that has four legs. I told her a snake. Honestly. Why does the residence have to treat us as if we're imbeciles, just because we're old? My youngest son, Armand, is the bright spot. We have a laugh if he visits without that wife... Suzanne?—No—Susan. We laugh because, of my four sons, Armand is the only one not enrolled in an eternal quest for the business deal of the century.

The air in here—it's as if we are walking to the cafeteria and the bingo room in a warm vapour of piss... augh, *la puanteur*... Not that the place isn't clean. Madame Sept-Petits-Bars bumps past every morning at five minutes past nine with her Electrolux, the poor woman is always getting its hose tangled, she trips over it and then it bangs into the walls... *quelle vacarme*! This week I'm coping by reading the autobiography of Gabrielle Roy—hardly cheerful, I know. I've been trying to get one of my older sons, André or Gilles, to show me how to operate the flatscreen TV they bought me, but they haven't had time. The thing takes up a quarter of my room, its useless lights flashing all night... I had to throw my dressing gown over it. And now Madame Poirer is coming to live here, *très jolie*, as if we've been lifelong confidantes. She's telephoned me every morning this week, wanting to know ridiculous details... Amandine! Are there buses to take us to

Bowling LeClerc? Do staff members meddle with one's correspondence? Is the food sufficient in *les enzymes alimentaires*?

No, Madame Poirer, suddenly my close friend, there are no buses because how can the staff take 275 of us out? There'll be no bowling here, and no *crème glacée* at Le Glacier Dillon on Rue Rivard. Last week two twenty-dollar bills disappeared from my room, and no, the food has no enzymes… Come on, Armand. It's noon. That's the thing about Armand, you can't rely on him to be on time. Not for any bad reason—stopping on the roadside… last time it was because he picked me the… fluffy… those branches with the new springtime… *les minous*. And another time he said he was collecting *les aiguilles* from a… a dead *porc-épic* for someone he knows to make a necklace… Suzanne must… *Susan* must love that. But what I love is that Armand reminds me of things I thought I'd forgotten. Do you remember this, Maman? Do you remember that?

Last time it was, "Do you remember Madame Poirer's dog?"

We dipped celery and… *les radis rouge*… in salt. I love the real *sel marin de Bretagne*. They harvest it in by hand. Here they give me a… *c'est horrible*… *une poussière noire*… made of seaweed granules! I throw it down the toilet. Armand escapes his wife in Montreal and he brings *sel de Guérande* and we dip the radishes. Suzanne, Susan, is intelligent but not sensible. She has no idea my youngest son can never thrive in the city. She thinks she has him broken in but my boy loves the country more than she—*pauvre* Suzanne… I tried to teach her, when she married him, how to look out for certain things, but she's one of those women who believe if men are stupid enough not to check their pockets for fifty-dollar bills before they go to the laundromat, then that is the men's own problem. Really, I find her *incompréhensible*.

"I *do* remember that dog," I told Armand. The celery was cold, the radishes bitter, and the salt had *flavour*. "Even before she got that dog, Madame Poirer was dog crazy. I remember we were at Le Glacier Dillon and a dog barked across the terrace and its owner bought it a cone. When I gave my opinion on people treating dogs like real children you'd think I had personally insulted Madame Poirer. Oh, she disliked me that day!"

Madame Poirer and her husband began poor. Well, we all did. But her husband started driving a school bus. Soon he had a whole fleet of buses, and he made a fair amount of money with that, then he opened a shop. He was not the smartest of men. He was naïve. But he managed his little business all right. He and Marcelle began to think more highly of themselves. Madame Poirer became a snob—she ordered a new living room set from Dupuis Frères on Rue Ste. Catherine, everything upholstered in red moquette bouclé. Then they sold their truck and bought themselves a brown Mercedes. Her children were suddenly more intelligent than anyone else's children—then she acquired that little dog.

"Armand, what was that dog's name?"

We had a dog ourselves, a dog my husband had named Alphonse Daudet, after the French writer.

"Nanette?"

"No. It was ... I think it was ... Dentelle?"

"That's it. A frilly dog."

Armand can bring the past to me in a way my other sons do not. When Armand was born, he weighed three pounds. You'd never guess this now. In those days, a three-pound baby did not always survive.

People come and go at a great rate here. Last week Monsieur Paquin died. Again, Armand had me laughing very ... *il m'a fait rire bruyamment* ... though I felt sad about Monsieur

Paquin—I mean I've danced with him. Armand reminded me Monsieur Paquin once had an apple stall.

"Remember," Armand found us egg sandwiches at the funeral reception even though Madame Sept-Petits-Bars had told me there were only tuna left, "what Monsieur Paquin told me about packing apples?"

When Armand was small, he sold Monsieur Paquin's apples door to door in a cart. Each morning—he was about ten years old—he took the apples from crates and put them in bags. Armand looked so cute wheeling his little go-cart.

"He told you no one will notice if you put one bruised apple in the bag, but if you put two in, they're sure to say something."

"That's right. He put one soft apple into every single bag he ever sold."

"You could rely on it."

After Armand told Susan that story she treated poor Monsieur Paquin like ... *elle lui a snobé* when she saw him coming and going in these halls, on her infrequent visits. Over apples he sold almost half a century ago. Do you see what I mean about my son's wife? There are a lot worse things a man can do than put one rotten apple in every bag. She's something of a dreamer, that one. She imagines my son can live with her for the rest of his life in the city. She has *absolument ... aucune idée ...* none at all, that Monsieur Paquin's habit of cheating his customers with the apples is funny.

Armand opened a tin of cashews. "Madame Poirer's dog was named Dentelle, and it was forbidden to leave home." We both knew our dog, Alphonse Daudet, had the run of the entire town of Abercorn. There was no place in town off limits to Alphonse Daudet. "And—do you remember, Maman, that Madame Poirer put a chastity belt on it?"

A chastity belt! Who knew there was such a thing for dogs? But I suppose if you're going to drive a Mercedes and name a dog Dentelle...

The cashews are something I like to keep on hand. When my older sons visit, it's all business. It's about my bills being paid, and my signature giving power of attorney to the eldest if I happen to wake up thinking a snake has four legs, and arrangements to do with extra services. They think I need the staff to look in on me more often. The staff mean well but they're all from tiny villages: Sainte-Émélie-de-l'Énergie or St. Joachim des Monts. Madame Carré with her homemade hat, and Madame Sept-Petits-Bars, the one with the vacuum cleaner—her real name is Madame Tichoux, little cabbage... she's a little cabbage all right, poor thing. All I needed was the measurement for something I wanted to frame, a special little card with a medal on it from my school days at L'École Normale.

"*C'est cinq pousses*, Madame DeLorimier," said the little cabbage—five inches—"and..." she frowned at her *ruban*, "*sept petits bars?*" Seven little bars—this was her term for seven sixteenths of an inch. I told this to Armand and he is the one who began calling her Madame Sept-Petits-Bars.

My older sons don't take me to Walmart, or buy small stepladders so I can climb into their passenger seats, or drive me over the Vermont border to see the magnificence of the leaves. Armand and I go to Tim Hortons, where I have chicken noodle soup, then we go to Walmart and I stock up on my cashews, and on M&M's for my grand-children, and cotton underwear, which keeps disappearing from my room along with the twenty-dollar bills and being replaced by disposable culottes. Armand never washes his van. I've given him money in an envelope and told him to go to a car wash.

Armand said, "But Madame Poirer discovered Alphonse Daudet had jumped through her laundry room window, do you remember, Maman? And he'd torn the chastity belt off Dentelle."

"Yes, she caught Alphonse Daudet mounting Dentelle underneath the ironing board."

Armand can never find a parking space close to Walmart's door, so he lets me off and I wait. I lean on my stick. There are times I have to wait ten minutes, the parking lots are so full. While I'm waiting I look at young people go by, and sometimes I wish I had that old photograph of myself, the one of my first day at my stenography position before I became a teacher—in high heels and lipstick at my typewriter—I would show it to … well, who on their way to Walmart would want to look? What clairvoyant stranger? Am I deluded as well as vain?

There was a bakery in Vermont where we all used to get peanut butter pie. The bakery had a worker who looked at me and flashed a … *un coup de foudre*. Every time, until one day—I don't know what happened—maybe I skipped a summer or something died in him, or in me, but one day he was no longer generous with his attention. He was no younger than I was, but he didn't want to waste it on me a second longer. I saw him flirt with a younger woman. Much younger than himself, but is life fair?

Armand brings me something … not the old days or their romance, but … there's an ointment my husband used to put on the … *sur les mamelles* … of our cows. What *is* that ugly word … udders! It came in a yellow tin. Romance departed and its spot gaped raw—I wouldn't tell this to just anyone— and nothing came to heal it. That's old age for you. But the laughter Armand brings me is salve on that spot.

"And Madame Poirer took Dentelle to the vet to have the dog's pregnancy … *terminé.*"

"I never knew that, Maman."

"And then one of her intelligent sons let Alphonse Daudet through the basement door with Dentelle again."

I've asked Madame Sept-Petits-Bars to inform her colleagues in the dining hall that liver makes me ... *j'en ai mal au coeur de ça.* When liver's on the menu they serve me chicken. I pay ten dollars extra on days Armand dines with me. On those days I don't eat with Madame Lefevre and Madame Pitre—they understand. My other sons never eat here. André is busy at IBM and Gilles says he detests the food. But according to Armand's Susan, what the brothers really mind is that everyone here is *décrépit.* There's a truth to that. It's no big news. All the residents are sick of looking at each other for that very reason. But Susan has no idea Armand tells me the things she says. She's a woman who tries to legislate who tells what to whom. That's what I mean by telling you she's a dreamer. Armand smuggles her cat in here. There's a strict policy against animals, but he stuffs the cat in his hockey bag, brings it up the elevator, and lays it in my lap where he lets it lick *la crème* of a pecan tart from his finger.

"Madame Poirer took her dog back to the vet," I told Armand. "*Elle l'avait stérilisé* ... but this time it died. She was glad to be done with that dog once and for all."... I wanted to continue, "But Armand, what am I going to do? She's coming here expecting me to act like an old friend ... will she expect to sit with me at the table I share with Madame Lefevre and Madame Pitre, where we sit as if we were at a fairly nice hotel, although it is hard to keep up the pretense at times—Madame Poirer is sure to make observations about aspects of the residence we choose to ignore. Having her at our table will ... *elle va perturber le statu quo ...*"

But I have never whined as an adult, and I'm not going to start now. Do you want to know when I realized, once and for all, that it does no good to lament? It has to do with that little medal for which I wanted Madame Sept-Petits-Bars to measure a frame. It was my school prize when I was sixteen. They give it to one graduating student each year at L'École Normale. I couldn't wait for my parents to come to the assembly. The *directrice* had told me I was the student to be honoured that year. I was so proud. We were all dying to see our parents, because we saw them only at Christmas and at the year-end. One of my sisters, Marguerite, cried for the first three months she was there. But my parents didn't show up. I don't know why. My father would come, I was sure of it—to see me crowned with La Médaille du Lieutenant-Gouverneur du Québec—but he didn't come. I took the buggy and the train home by myself, and no one mentioned my medal. The only reason I want it framed now is that my oldest son said he wouldn't mind having it. So I realized, when I was sixteen, it's no use to feel sorry for yourself. *Il est absolument futile.*

So I keep my dread of Madame Poirer to myself. Armand has problems of his own, with that Susan. He keeps his socks in their basement because she feels he has too many pairs. To please her, he has gathered them in a garbage bag and carted them downstairs. Each morning he has to go in the basement to get his socks. The wife told me this. She believes she is telling me fondly and we'll laugh about it together, two women who supposedly love my son. But she has no idea how to laugh with me. And does she love him? I wonder about it. For her, everything has to be explained or it doesn't deserve to exist, and how can Armand be explained? What kind of life does he have with her? She's the kind of woman who wouldn't have a clue how to enjoy the story of Madame Poirer's dog without asking for details nobody cares about: "What exactly does it look like, a chastity belt for dogs... is it hand-knotted or do you buckle it?" Everything is official with her—I remember the time she began to ask me about the death of my husband, which happened in Morocco—he was on a bus trip and I didn't go. Well Susan made an interrogation of it: was it a *crise cardiaque*, or was it an *anévrisme*? And how did I find out? And how did I feel at the time?

How did she think I felt? And when I happened to mention that he did not return home—they were not able to send his body here by airplane until three months had passed—well that was a mystery for Monsieur Sherlock Holmes in her opinion.

"Three months? Why three months?"

"Because they had to prepare his body in the Moroccan way, in the way they had then, at that time..."

"What way was that? What do you mean?" Her eyes were like wheels. It was as if I'd told her my husband had run off on some kind of wild escapade.

When I told her they dried him, that's how they preserved corpses, she interrupted, "How did you know it was him?" as if there must have been a mistake. I explained that I had sent for his brothers, who confirmed it was Joseph. "Armand never told me this," she protested, "Why wouldn't Armand tell me this about his father's death?" Maybe Armand didn't know, I said—he was only sixteen when it happened. Well, you should have seen her then—to her, the story should have gone down as some sort of family heirloom; our own *Les Mille et une Nuits*; not just the death of Joseph, my ordinary husband, who happened to be on a holiday.

I had better warn Armand not to mention Madame Poirer to Susan at all, or she'll invite the woman here to elaborate on the chastity belt over a nice cup of tea and I'll never get rid of... "So happy to see you with your old friend... How marvellous that life is never a dead end but a spiral... and now you needn't feel alone on the days Armand can't come..." Yes, that's her...

marvellous... and that grating voice of Madame Poirer... I can hear the two of them now, crowding me out of my own room, driving me out on the balcony with its dead spider plant and its view of the exhaust fan on the roof of that takeout next door, some kind of Arabic snack bar, from which stream enticing young men—*beaux jeunes hommes*—devouring delicious-looking shish kebabs. I dream sometimes of descending the fire escape and enjoying my lunch there among them, messy shreds of lettuce and onions *en cascade, agneau brûlé* dripping with juice... Do you know what Susan doesn't know? You wake up one morning, oh yes, Susan, it will get you too—you wake up to find, completely unknown to you before that day, six inches from your face there has somehow loomed a brick wall. Can't you sense it in the distance? .

FLYAWAY

THERE WAS A CHILD AT THE HEAD of the procession with a nest of flyaway hair on her head and out of all the evacuees coming from Shields and Hebburn and Newcastle I knew that she was the one they were going to give me to look after. Me, aged seventy-six, never married, never had my own child. This one glared over my gate and I knew she didn't want me. She wanted the Heslops across the road with their collie and seven kids, but she wasn't going to get them. You never got what you wanted in the war. I never wanted to open up my house, the house I'd shared with Cinders and before that other cats, forty-seven years, since my own mother died. Oh you should have seen the way the authorities peeled this child away from the procession and nudged her through my garden. Her head was down and she was ill-dressed—her mother must've sewn that knapsack out of an old blanket, blue with fringes, and her stockings were rolled around her ankles in bulges—there was something gruesome and familiar about those stockings—I wondered why she had to wear them in summer. And eat! All that child wanted to do, all she ever talked about, was eat. Where did she think I was going to get bread and milk and raisins and ham in the middle of the war? Really, did they give us enough money to look after these children, and did anyone ask us how we felt? You just had to put up with it; if you said anything you were ungrateful and you weren't doing your part. Gracie, that was her name, and I felt no natural affection for her and she felt none for me. But we tolerated each other. We had to, didn't we.

She was five when she came to me, and her mother was old. Her mother was forty and she worked in the munitions factory in Workington and we saw her only every third or fourth weekend. I don't know what was worse, the mother coming or not coming. If the mother had come more often, things might not have happened the way they did.

I don't know what kind of house the pair had lived in in Shields, but they seemed frightened of what they called the country. I didn't live in the country, I lived on a residential street in Seaton, but they had it in their heads that because there was grass to walk on, we were in an alarming wilderness. The child, Gracie, kept her head down the first three weeks. The place was so green and bright she said it hurt her eyes, and at first she was deathly afraid of my cat just because it caught birds and brought them home in its mouth, the way cats do.

"Why has Cinders got a bleeding bird in his mouth?" she asked.

"Because it's food. You eat chicken, don't you? A chicken's a bird. A cat will never go hungry."

"Won't it?"

"It will always find a meal somewhere. And Cinders is not a he. Cinders is a lady cat. She's going to have babies soon."

"Kittens!"

"And I'm going to have to drown them in a bucket."

The child and her mother must have lived on one of those paved streets in Shields with no plumbing and Roman ruins— the mother mentioned the ruins as if they were something special—and no trees unless you walked to someplace they called Seaview Terrace. This child tried to evade the sight of grass and trees, though I made her go outside every day to get her used to the surroundings.

Having a child in your house when you're elderly is a most trying exercise. A child constantly wants a fairground of some sort, a game, a lollipop, some entertainment. I had never considered my days uneventful or oppressive until that child came into them, but when she sat there in her one skirt, the only skirt in her little sack, day after day, staring at my chairs and carpet and curtains with a pathetic face, I was at my wits' end thinking of something to get her out of my way. I didn't want her to play with the Heslop children across the road because I have not forgotten what that family was like when I was a child, and I didn't like the things they said about me now. I didn't want to have to go over there looking for Gracie and therefore having to encounter that family or have them look at me in the way they did. The thought of it tired me, as did most things. At seventy-six a frail person can be easily tired, and wants quietness. Some people my age can still barge around at full strength, but I can't, and that's just the way it is. I could have pleaded illness to avoid having this evacuee, Gracie, come to my house, and perhaps that's what I should have done. I might have got Doctor Whitfield to write a note saying I had long suffered from ... how do people put it? Something ridiculous ... *circadian disruption* ... but when the call came for guardians I somehow forgot children don't sit in one place all day and behave themselves. I forgot they're unlike the doll I lost long ago, the doll who behaved herself and did nothing but drink pretend tea out of a toy pot I kept refilling from a jug my mother kept for me to play with before our accident. My doll's name was Tilly, short for Mathilda, and she formed the extent of what I know about looking after anybody, and look what happened to her.

The personality of the wild-haired child was, I might have to say, devious. She didn't look for food when I was watching, but if I lay on my bed for a rest, she'd prowl in the pantry, lifting my saucer off the gooseberry jam, sticking her finger in it and licking that finger and sticking it in the jam again. Odious. She was like a mouse with the bread—I'd find the loaf crumbled round the edges where she'd pilfered morsels. I had a crock in which I kept bacon when I was lucky enough to get it from Gerald Bell who keeps a few pigs down the lane, and I know she tore strips of fat off that to eat. This was in addition to bread and herring and raspberries I gave her at noon, sufficient for my sustenance but evidently not for hers. Bread was hard to get, and even the raspberries and gooseberries were scarce, as it was almost impossible not to have them stolen by the Heslop children unless I watched constantly out the window, and who can be vigilant forever? I was overcome by tiredness daily by two in the afternoon, and it was during these afternoon naps that my berries were stolen and other things went wrong.

The first time the milk disappeared I thought Gracie must have drunk it and hidden the bottle. But she wasn't around. Bluebells had made her overcome her fear of the lanes and she gathered bunches that she expected me to put in a jam jar on the sill, so I thought she must be gathering more. But she didn't come home at five for her tea. Five on the dot, she'd normally pipe up, "My tummy's rumbling, Miss Penrice," and I felt the tiresome obligation of it most heavily. But by six on this day she hadn't come home. I loathed having to do it but I went and knocked on the Heslops' door and she wasn't there either.

At first Mrs. Heslop seemed too distracted to even remember I had Gracie living with me. With seven children and her own evacuee I wasn't surprised. When I insisted she asked did I want to come in and wait until their Terry and Beverley came home and see if they knew anything. No thank you, I said, I'm sure she'll come home on her own. Then Brian came running down the stairs, the youngest, and he said, "I know how to find her!" but his mother shushed him and told me to pay no attention,

"Brian's always making things up." she said. "You cannot trust a thing he says…" So I went back home and waited.

I remember part of me felt a little bit excited that maybe this was it, the end of Gracie, and me having responsibility for her. Nobody would be able to blame me for losing her—no one expected a seventy-six-year-old guardian to be able to follow a child's every step. Maybe she'd had an accident like the one I had when I was her age. Or maybe she'd been what is called stolen by the fairies. Every village has that happen once or twice in a generation. I suppose those stolen children are really stolen by tinkers or gypsies or what have you… in any case, no one expects an old woman to be able to counteract these things, which are facts of life in any town or city or village no matter what the size, and it's nobody's fault.

But what was I to do next? What was the procedure for the guardian of an evacuated child if harm befell the child or the child went missing? Hadn't we had all been sent notices months before, the bureau of this or that, a name and address of someone to call… but what had I done with mine? I searched the sideboard among the bills and deeds and what have you, but I didn't find it, nor was it in my bedroom, and it occurred to me that even if I found the document with some name on it, a Mrs. Davis or Mrs. Ostle—I fancy it was a Mrs. and not a Mr.—what good would it do me to write them a letter? A letter would take time to reach that Mrs. Somebody, then they'd have to respond, and there was no way such a correspondence would have any effect on what might have befallen Gracie tonight… but why did I feel an exultant leap?… If Gracie didn't come home by nine o'clock, I decided, I'd walk to Bramley's Dry Goods and get Mrs. Bramley to find a policeman. At least people would say I had looked for her.

But Gracie tumbled home at dusk.

"Where have you been?"

"Finding things to eat."

"Is eating all you think about?"

"… No."

"Yes it is. What did you find?"

"Spiky things hanging down, then sausage rolls."

"Who gave you those?"

"A bird and a man."

She did not ask for food and never mentioned hunger from that night on. Then on a Monday the child and the milk disappeared again, and I also realized I hadn't seen Cinders for some time, and that she must have had her kittens. I convinced myself Gracie was taking the milk to feed Cinders and the kittens in some hiding place, and I felt betrayed by my cat, though I know cats are hardly loyal creatures. Again Gracie came home at nightfall and didn't sneak any bread from the pantry.

Gracie's mother was uppity for someone with a child so down-at-heel, and looked down-at-heel herself, for that matter, except that there was something about the mother's hair and her skin and her eyes and her bearing that said don't you dare look down on me. She had defiant eyes and somehow managed to keep her hair in what they call a Marcelle wave. For a woman with a child whose knapsack was sewn out of an old blanket, and whose own clothing was threadbare, she acted haughtily. "Gracie looks," she charged on one of her weekend visits, "underweight. She looks as if she is not eating enough. Are you sure she is getting enough at mealtimes?"

"Indeed she is. There is no want of herring or bread or gooseberry jam here."

"That skin on her knee…"

"She fell in the lane. It's impossible for me to keep up with her, or to stop her from racing around. She fell and little stones got embedded in the skin, and ..."

"All the same, it was that way two weeks ago, and it looks no better." The woman handed me a jar of rosehip syrup from the chemist. "Give her a teaspoon of this every morning and before bedtime. She's run down, for her knee to look like that. She needs vitamins. If this weren't the weekend I would take her to the doctor myself. In fact, where does the doctor live?" She asked this imperiously, and took the child that very afternoon to Gale Terrace and interrupted Doctor Whitfield's Sunday dinner, and when she came back she said Gracie had impetigo and I must do some nursing care. Anything to do with sores or bandages can make me faint, but the haughty manner of this woman prevented me from saying so.

"You will get," she said carefully, "an extra five shillings a week for your diligence until the knee is healed. And why hasn't she got her woolen stockings on?"

I remembered the loathsome objects. "Aren't woolen stockings in summer far too hot?"

The mother persisted in her haughty tolerance. She was the real mother and I was an inferior substitute. "Have you never heard of diphtheria, Mrs. Penrice? Gracie had it when she was two."

"But why does she have to wear them now? I mean, it's summer ... they're ... itchy and ..."

"After the diphtheria, she had scarlet fever. She was in the hospital for weeks and I was afraid I might never see her again. They told me, when they let her come home with me, that I had to be militant against draughts."

"Oh ... I remember ..."

"You remember what?"

But I didn't want to tell her. I remembered now, long ago ... my own mother making me wear the very same kind of stockings though none of my friends had to wear anything of the sort.

The woman looked about to challenge me some more, but I think she feared I might retaliate during the long weeks she was away from her child, working in the shell factory. "Give her this," she said, producing something I hadn't seen since before the war. I don't know where that woman got a hold of a parkin made with ginger and treacle in wartime, and that night I devoured it with a cup of Typhoo.

"Tell your mother the parkin was lovely," I told Gracie. "Say nothing about the bird and the man giving you things to eat." But I never could tell whether Gracie obeyed because I told her to, or for reasons peculiar to her own tendencies toward subterfuge and deceit.

The next time Gracie disappeared I waited by my gate until I saw little Brian Heslop crawl under the brambles to find his dog's chewed ball. I knew how thoroughly it was chewed, and how slimy it was, since it was in my hand. But its slime didn't bother me. I was remembering the day he told his mother he knew how to find Gracie, and his mother shushing him.

"Here it is," I waved the nasty ball. "I'll give it to you if you promise to help me find out two things."

"What things?"

"Remember how you knew where Gracie went, the day she was lost?"

"Ma wouldn't let me tell."

"And who's stealing milk from my doorstep and giving it to the mother cat? Tell me and I'll give you your ball back, and ... a slice of bread and gooseberry jam."

"I'm sick of gooseberry jam. Have you not got any treacle tart?"

"You cheeky thing." I put the ball in my pinny pocket.

"Gracie climbs up Amos Graham's beech tree and picks the nuts and eats them, then she goes to the back of Holliday's Butcher and Jimmy who drives the wagon gives her two stale sausage rolls..." Fast as the River Seaton after the rain in April he tumbled out with it... "She gives one to Cinders and eats the other one then she slurps the cream off your milk and gives Cinders the rest in a Smedleys pie tin. Then she crawls in Max Dockerty's henhouse and finds two eggs and she goes up the road to Mrs. Litster's house and Mrs. Litster fries one egg and puts it in a sandwich and gives it to Gracie..." On and on, did his concoctions have no end? "... and she keeps the other one for herself, and Max Dockerty doesn't care. Nobody cares because they all say Gracie's got to eat something and you don't give her hardly nothing at all because you've never been right in the head. My ma says next time Gracie's mam comes she's gonna tell on you. She's gonna tell her you give Gracie nothing but rotten herring and hard gooseberries. She says she should've told her ages ago but then you wouldn't get your eight shillings and sixpence every week and god knows what you might say about her and then my ma might lose her billet money as well... She says you're cracked as a pisspot."

"Little blighter, pull the other one. Your mother told me you never stop making up stories..."

"You're the one who makes up stories... everyone says you're barmy. Everyone says you were never right in the head since you fell down the well when you were little. That's why... gimme my ball!"

It is true I fell down the well. Was I eight? I remember gulping, then inhaling the cold water... thrashing... sinking... then it felt lovely... I kept tight hold of my doll, Mathilda... she went in the well with me so it was both of us together... and then I lost her, and I was in my bed... bed that whole summer... but what had the boy called me? People were so ... they were too loud. Shouting and rushing around ...

"And that's why you never got married."

"I didn't want to get married. I never wanted ..."

How people interpreted things. Here I was, a quiet person to whom marriage and men and husbands seemed brutal... yet here was young Brian Heslop insinuating I'd rather be married than ... couldn't a person be quiet without being considered *not all there*? If it hadn't been so insulting it might have amused me. I'd become used to letting people think whatever they wanted as long as they left me alone. I'd been alone for years... but now, Gracie.

There was something in what little Brian Heslop said that shifted my feeling for Gracie, whom I'd regarded as a nuisance and an invader. Might she and I really be on the same side, different from everybody around here, with their raucous shouting and everything black and white with four corners... Gracie was a quiet child... why hadn't I appreciated her?

Quiet little Gracie, all independent, climbing Amos Graham's beech tree and devouring all his beechnuts! Why hadn't I realized Gracie meant beechnuts when she told me a bird had shown her food that was something spiky hanging down? Those beechnuts came back to me, swirling from my own childhood. I'd spent whole afternoons in that tree myself, when it belonged not to Amos but to his father William, and I'd picked those nuts and peeled off their spiny skin to collect the chewy meats inside, and I'd ... no wonder the child wasn't hungry. I feasted on those nuts when I was her age. They filled your belly right up. I never cared that my father said they were for pigs. Why did grown-ups have to spoil all the excitement? And sausage rolls! How I loved stealing sausage rolls my mother laid out to cool on the windowsill, piping hot, straight out of the oven with rivulets of juice bubbling out the knife-holes. What was wrong with grown-ups, wanting their sausage rolls cold? Poor Gracie, getting stale ones from that fellow who drove Hector Holliday's meat truck—what had Brian said his name was? Jimmy? But how clever... stealing Max Dockerty's eggs and then getting— of all people—Evelyn Litster to fry one up and stuff it in a sandwich!

The child was brilliant. I had not given her nearly enough credit, worrying as I'd begun to do, now that I'd grown old, about all those practical things I never cared a fig about when I was a child... No, I had been mistaken about Gracie. She rose in my estimation like a spear of sorrel by the lane, wild and just as surprising in her piquancy, yes, she was refreshing, and now I wanted to see her embarking on her resourceful little improvisations—the thought made something like childish joy spring up inside me for the first time since...

"My granddad was the one who lifted you out," Brian Heslop said now. "He was the only one of his brothers little enough to go down after you."

It was true. "They looped your granddad in a rope."

"And lowered him and he grabbed you and saved your life."

"He did. Freddy Heslop."

"But you were unconscious for ages and your brain went soft and it never went right again. But that's all right. You've got your house and Mam says you've got a nice little penchant."

"Pension."

"Yes. My mam says if she had a nice little penchant like yours she'd be all set and she wouldn't have to do scrubbing for the Davises and the Wilsons and my dad might never have run off with Mavis Abernethy..."

"That's enough. Your voice is too loud." I put my hand against my ears, the way I have to when I turn the radio on and it makes that awful crackling noise, or when I'm startled by a horde of crows all squawking at once.

"You're the one who's shouting, Mrs. Penrice. You're not even shouting, you're screaming."

I wanted no more of the Heslop child. I wanted to find my own child, the intriguing, resourceful girl from South Shields, exploring hidey-holes of the village like I'd done as a child when everything was still all right, before I nearly drowned. There was something lovely about her I'd failed to notice before: I'd focused on the milk, the herring, her wetting the bedsheets, instead of on the fact that she'd tried to bring my own childhood back, the happy part of it... all those bright memories.

"Scram now, you," I told Brian Heslop, and whipped his dog's ball at him as hard as I could, and set off for the back field where I'd walked all my life to gather beechnuts in the Grahams' tree.

When you're my age it takes longer to walk to that beech tree than it takes a child of Gracie's youth, and another thing, that tree has become larger and hard to recognize. Seeing it now, knowing Gracie's up in the branches, feels a bit like when I visit my mother's grave: that grave has become unrecognizable though it retains a familiar air. What I mean is that the day it was a fresh grave seems like yesterday, yet it's now covered in growth that looks ancient, because of course it is ancient. And it's the same with the beechnut tree. Was it not yesterday I was in the high branches like Gracie, picking nuts and eating them, hidden in the leaves, no one able to find me... "She's gone again," they said... "Gone, gone, gone... all day long in a world of her own."

And Gracie now, up there... lured by that same lovely tree... branches embracing her, feeding her, the only difference being that since the tree is bigger now, the child has climbed perilously high. Much higher than I was ever able to climb it... sky in her hair, and the sun so low her one little skirt is barely … is it her? Are those her legs and her feet solid on the branches … braced, but all the same … I feel dizzy.

"Gracie?"

I dare not call out too loud. No one understands the importance of speaking gently … is that … on the grass, my cat?

"Cinders?"

Her eyes flash in the gathering dusk—the cat glares at me and I remember it has been with Gracie for days: she has fed it, has helped it hide its kittens. The cat is a stranger to me. It doesn't even look like Cinders. I remember a thing my mother said about cats. They have nine lives, yes, but the lives are not consecutive. They have one life with you but eight other lives going on at the same time, about which you know nothing.

"Gracie …"

Not loud enough. For her to hear me, I'd have to shout, and I hate shouting, hate it. The branches are familiar: easy, at first, to climb—just like rungs on a ladder, at the start; that's what I always loved about this tree—it's only after the first four steps up it starts to … why must my legs insist on shaking? I've done this so many times. Stop quivering, legs! The bark is loose, or slippery … where's that crook where I always used to put my foot?

I've heard complaints that when some people grow old they do silly things, they forget they're no longer agile and behave in foolhardy ways. But I don't think it foolhardy for me to try to get a tiny bit closer to Gracie, to coax her back down. Dusk is … I don't want her to lose the light, or startle. Why have I not thought before now how easily she might startle? I've driven her from my house, eager to get rid of her, when I should have remembered how it feels to be young and small and not exactly loved. She's been a good little girl, really. She has to have been, for hasn't Cinders taken to her? Animals don't like unsympathetic people. Cats know who is gentle, who is on their side.

119

"Gracie?" I call from a crook in the low branches, inch my hand to the next fork, shake my slippers off… the best way to climb William Graham's beech tree has always been with bare feet. When Gracie can hear me the first thing I'll tell her will be to kick off her plimsolls. But purple darkens the sky and I know how one minute you think you can climb down the tree but the next you can't see the branch below you. If we don't descend together in the next few minutes…

"I want you to come down now… Gracie?"

The child has often pretended not to hear me and I wish I'd made a better rapport with her, because I have no way of knowing if she's listening now. If only I'd understood sooner what a brave little thing she is… My legs are rattling, the way they do when I stand too long on my stepladder trying to reach the rhubarb jam. I wish I could trust my legs but I can't. I wish that bloody Heslop boy were here to help. Panic's a funny thing: as long as you sweet-talk it, it's domestic and tame, but when night comes and the child is in the branches, so high, and you're old, it becomes an act of will to keep panic bound, and I exercise that will now, my legs and arms trembling. I remember being a child on roller skates on the downhill cobblestones and my legs felt like cushions full of pins and I have that same feeling now—it frightens me and when I see the bicycle light of Brian Heslop's older brother—Terrence or Trevor?—I have no choice but to cry out.

People are looking up—someone waves a lantern and for once they're murmuring quietly. I try to assure them I am not dangerously far up the tree, but the truth is I'm paralyzed. Really, I should be able to climb down by myself, if only I could remember where the supporting branches are and not the brittle ones. This lack of certainty makes me ashamed to have become old. The indignity enrages me. Now they're sending a man up the trunk—is it William Graham's son Amos? He looks like his father; his arm digs into my ribs—it hurts.

"The last time you did this, Mrs. Penrice, you promised never to do it again."

"But the girl …" It's awful how fright can make you hesitate. I want to warn him to get Gracie down first. Gracie, high in the tree … her slippery plimsolls. I forgot to notice if she's wearing those awful stockings. If she falls … but it's as if I'm in that dream where you strain to speak, yet cannot. "The little girl," I force it out.

So. I have spoken, however hoarsely, on Gracie's behalf. No one can say I haven't. I fear that because of the dark, and Gracie's silence—so furtive, but for good reason—no one will know she's in the topmost branches, stars winking over her head. She wants to remain quiet as a mouse until we've all gone back in our houses, then climb down on her own and sleep in Graham Bell's barn with Cinders and the kittens.

"She might fall," I manage to caution Amos Graham. Mrs. Heslop has rushed across the street with Brian and the older one with the bicycle, and I see their slavery dog, all their faces garish beneath the lantern the older boy swings high. "The little girl might fall." I crumple into Mrs. Heslop's arms and am ashamed that my tears wet her dress. I feel like a real fool. "Get the little girl down."

"Shh, shh," Mrs. Heslop says. "The little girl is all right."

"But I couldn't reach her and it's getting dark …"

"Never mind that now, shhh …"

"You'll get her down?"

"Don't worry, Mrs. Penrice. You don't need to worry about her any more."

But when they get me back into my house, I don't see Gracie. I see her mother. They must have telegraphed her and she must have come instantly. When I reach my house she's folding Gracie's pyjamas and her few little vests and I realize she's taking the things away and Gracie is already gone. The mother is going to let her board with her in the boarding house she rents in Workington. I see she's packing those cumbersome stockings, the loathsome wool things Gracie wore bunched around her ankles. The mother is folding those stockings as if they'll save her daughter from the war, from any danger of falling from beechnut trees, from diphtheria and scarlet fever, from everything that can befall a frail child on this earth. A mother's love is like that. That is where, I realize, a real mother falls short, into wishfulness and illusion, whereas we foster mothers of wartime, though we may not possess proper maternal feeling, come equipped with a far clearer and less romantic grasp on reality.

KNIVES

Was I a good neighbour?

I doubted I was a good sister-in-law: when all the Desmarais brothers told me brother number five was seeing a young woman named Marlene every Thursday night down at The Misty Moon, I toyed with the idea of telling Yvonne, his wife, in the name of sisterhood, but in the end I said nothing, just like everyone else. It subsequently became clear to me that Yvonne Desmarais had her own reasons for not caring: she knew all along about the affair and it helped rather than hurt her marriage.

But this thing with the neighbour, Eleanor Dickson, when it came to a head near Halloween when our boys were thirteen, well, I hated to be part of the subterfuge. If Eleanor had known a similar thing about my life, known it for years yet prattled on about July's strange hailstones or the new councillor with alopecia or the insane speed limit proposed for our street, and then I found out the thing she'd kept secret, I'd have wanted to strangle her.

Running in front of our houses was a poplar-lined skateboard feature that the town put in place for the kids. My son Joey and Eleanor Dickson's kids all went to St. Winnifred's school around the corner and when they came home, they got their boards and skates and played until dark. The problem was, my friend Joan Corlett sent her son Adam over here from across town on his stilts to sleep over at my place with Joey, so he did his circus tricks there all the time, on that strip, which happened to run right past Eleanor's house. Unbeknownst to Eleanor, at least I believed she was unaware, Adam Corlett was her husband Ed's illegitimate son.

According to Joan, Adam had been conceived fourteen summers before in Margaree where Joan was working on an episode of some pilot about rumrunners and Vikings. Joan was thirty-nine then and had no interest in a husband but a very big interest in having a kid, when who should show up in Margaree Harbour but just the kind of no good bad-boots Joan liked to sleep with: a pack of Export A tucked in his sleeve, lightning ascent up the scaffold on which he was replacing siding on the inn where Joan just happened to have a very comfortable and lonely suite. I barely knew Joan then, but I know she was aware Edward Dickson had a pregnant wife—Eleanor—and a toddler back in Halifax, but what was that to Joan Corlett or her famished uterus and beetle-hard manicure.

Joan kept her hair cut like the red hair of that famous New York fashion what's-her-name, Anna Wintour, and she had a hard little face men somehow managed to go crazy over, although I suppose it could have been other things they liked—at Justin Thyme Deli I overheard the president of the Board of Trade say she had a nice rack on her. Did he mean like antlers on a game animal? How are breasts like antlers? I never know what people mean when they use popular terminology. Joan was from the Isle of Man. She had a soft accent but to me her hardness superseded it and I would not have wanted to be one of the men she ate alive.

So her son Adam grew to live and breathe stilts and hacky sacks and juggling sticks—what were they called?—devil or diabolo sticks. He was agile like Ed Dickson and was recruited as a sort of extra in a couple of circus shows when Cirque du Soleil came to town. That was how my son Joey became friends with Adam, and it was also when Joan started sending Adam to sleep over at our place when she went out of town. We both knew I lived four doors down from Ed Dickson. Sometimes I wondered if that fact excited Joan.

I found the mind of Joan Corlett fascinating and treacherous. She made sure her son and his secret father spent clandestine time together. She told me she dropped Adam off at Caravaggio's Restaurant downtown once a month to have lunch with Ed so that Ed could keep abreast of events in the life of his son. Adam Corlett had a bit of a rough time at school, tripping teachers on the stairs and accidentally setting fire to things. I found it hard to believe Ed Dickson was not also keeping abreast of Joan. But what amazed me the most was that in a compact downtown like ours it never seemed to worry Ed Dickson that someone he or his wife Eleanor knew might see him sharing calamari with Adam Corlett, his secret child. It seemed to me like an arrangement crying out to be exposed.

Adam was serious about his circus manoeuvres and came over more and more often, forever sending objects or himself flying in front of the houses on our side of the street, sleeping over whenever Joan went on a shoot in Rockport, Maine or Cape Breton and wherever else she went, up on rooftops half the time, and on cranes or interviewing crews on Spanish trawlers—you could never keep track of Joan.

The night it all came apart I was having one of my kitchen sales. I held them every October and closer to Christmas I sold fair trade craft items made by women and their daughters in developing countries, and I had other sales as well. It was a bit of extra income and an excuse to have a social. But this time Ed's wife Eleanor was coming over, and Adam Corlett was sleeping over as well, and I was worried. The two had never been in my house at the same time. It was late October: people had hung witches and ghosts on their doors, they hung plastic pumpkins lit up in the poplars and hedges, and my son Joey wore his sweater with the skeleton on it. I was afraid I might let something slip in front of Eleanor Dickson with Adam right there in the house—I can knock back a few too many glasses of Chardonnay if I'm not counting—I was also wary about Adam: he was an unpredictable kid. I felt a sorry fondness for him … his hair flopped over a face that had soft edges, and it was too bad, I thought, that any boy should have to pretend he did not have a father when he knew that father lived in the same town and had three other children he took to hockey practices and all the other things dads do. I invited my friend Maurice over to help me prepare for the sale and give me advice on whether to try and keep the boys upstairs and out of sight or what. Maurice knew the whole story of Adam Corlett's secret father. A lot of us did.

This particular kitchenware sale was all about knives: I had new avocado slicers and a corrugated carrot knife and some heavy-duty blades for carving beef, and a couple of sushi blades and some high-end pieces I didn't expect to sell because the neighbours I invited usually went for the stuff between twenty and forty-five dollars, but the company insisted I show samples of every price range.

Maurice helped me mix smoked paprika dip and Mexican relish. "The kid…" he folded chopped olives into cream cheese…

"Adam."

"Has he *seen* Eleanor Dickson before?"

"That's a good question."

"I mean he knows Ed is his father—you told me about the monthly lunches…"

"Shh—not too loud, Maurice. Adam's upstairs now with Joey."

"I know, I hear them—what a racket. What are they doing, flinging those devil sticks from one end of the hall to the other?"

"Here, take these breadknives and arrange them on that board, Eleanor's bringing baguettes for demonstrating… I told her not to go to any trouble but you know what she's like…"

"Is she bringing her homeless brother?"

"She might. She said Ed doesn't want to be home alone with him. He drives Ed insane." The homeless brother, Leon, had just shown up on Eleanor's doorstep for his annual fortnight of sleeping on Eleanor's couch, devouring her damson crumble and shoplifting at the Mic Mac Mall. "He worries Eleanor to distraction but she's too kind a soul to say a word… Can you please put those grape knives with the grapes?"

"So the stilt kid…"

"Adam."

"He *knows* Ed lives practically next door to you, in the house he totters past on those stilts, back and forth like a pendulum, like a dashboard dog…"

"Yes, Adam knows. Keep your voice down!"

"The way he parades in front of their house on those stilts it's almost as if he *wants*…"

"Shh!"

"Or *she* wants… his mother…"

"Don't ask me to decipher the mind of Joan Corlett."

"Eleanor must have seen Adam before, on her steps or in her driveway… he's gone past her front window on those stilts a thousand times." Maurice helped me arrange the grape peelers, the grapefruit knives that were more like spoons, the cheese slicers and Thai cleavers, and the special one… "Where's the other stuff you usually sell? The greeting cards painted by people who hold the paintbrushes in their mouths?"

"That's at Christmas. This is kitchenware, and tonight it's all knives."

"So I see." He picked the special one up and dangled it. "What's this snazzy specimen?"

"That's my *pièce de résistance* tonight. It's called a Wa-Gyuto. Japanese. Nice, hey?"

"How much?"

"Two hundred and thirty-six dollars."

"Holy snapping arseholes, Marguerite." This was a thing the straight boys used to say when Maurice and I were in junior high, a million years ago, and Maurice used to mimic them.

"Watch your tongue, Maurice. Eleanor's lovely, handsome homeless brother might be put off by that kind of language and you're always saying how you'd like to meet a man who is dangerous but also elegant."

People started arriving. I felt dread and anticipation whenever the door opened to let in a blast of October night. Would the evening be a success? I knew my sales were hardly profound get-togethers but they were an excuse to party at the darkening part of the year and eat salty, fatty snacks. I always invited Darlene and Greta, whose mission in life was to keep any conversation from turning serious. Darlene arrived in red go-go boots and Greta brought a whoopee cushion and tucked it under the rear end of each new arrival as they sat down. Eleanor arrived with her homeless brother who was beautiful in a brooding, semi-schizophrenic poet way, the kind of person I can get talking to about the meaning of life, after a few glasses of wine. He had Jesus-clear eyes and was unfazed to enter a room full of women who saw him—as they saw Maurice—as if he were a cat instead of a man. I saw why he'd drive Ed Dickson nuts—right about now Ed would be ramping up the gears on his treadmill in front of *Hockey Night in Canada*.

Just as Eleanor arrived, the boys, Adam Corlett and my Joey, thundered downstairs to swarm the snack table. I handed them a box of Ritz and a bag of mallow puffs and hissed, "Get back upstairs."

"Are those the ones with jam in them?" Joey bit a cookie and scowled.

"Whoooooa look at these blades..." Adam Corlett lifted a cleaver and watched it glitter impressively under my halogen fixtures. "I can practise being Ramo Samee!"

"Do you know how sharp that is?" I grabbed his wrist, uncurled his fingers from the handle and held the knife out of his reach. "Go on—you, Joey—get back upstairs and don't even *think* about touching the knives."

"I *hate* the ones with no jam!" Joey reached for a pumpkin seed cracker and dug at the Mexican dip. "I want to stay down here."

"Come *on*." Adam tugged Joey's sweater. "I've got an ancient Indian trick up my sleeve..."

"Yes," I gave Joey a shove I would later regret. "Get out of here, you two. You're not interested in *Collecting the Regalia*."

"Nobody is," interjected the always-helpful Maurice. "Who the hell is Ramo Samee?"

"Collecting the what?" piped up Greta.

"*Collecting the Regalia*," said Maurice, "is Marguerite's party game that she found cut out of an ancient copy of *The Daily Mail* and stored in her great-aunt Mildred's chocolate box. It involves passing bits of paper folded up with the crown jewels or something written on them..."

"*Crown, Sceptre* and *Sword*," I corrected him. "The first person to collect the whole set wins a..."

"We played it last year," Darlene told Greta. "You had ringworm and couldn't come. I won fishnet stay-ups. I wore them to work and they fell down."

"Ramo Samee was, I believe, a Victorian sword-swallower," said the homeless brother of Eleanor, quietly into my ear, as Adam Corlett dragged Joey upstairs and Maurice reluctantly began passing the Cadbury box full of folded sceptres and orbs. "From the Far East." His voice made me wish I had on a decent pair of fishnets instead of my merino tights. I knew I had better get the green graph paper off the table before I drank any more wine, so I could write down the knife orders. Maybe Maurice could do the writing… there he was, inspecting the knife display… was he mouthing something at me across the room?

"What?"

"Where's the Wa-Gyuto?"

"It should be there."

"The Wa-Gyuto…" louder this time. "appears to have gone."

"Gone?" Eleanor Dickson sat up straight. "Has something gone?" Her voice high and sharp.

"The Japanese knife," said Maurice. "Marguerite's *pièce de résistance*…"

Eleanor sprang up as if she were personally responsible and started shifting platters around, searching under their rims. I realized she was glaring at her homeless brother.

"Leon?" Eleanor strode over to him. "We need to talk outside." She dragged him out through the front door, Leon patient and forbearing.

Darlene kicked her boots off, dug her knees in my cushions made of sari silk, and jammed her face between the curtains. "They're huddled on your steps having some sort of a…"

From upstairs came a drawn-out and bloodcurdling scream.

"… confab… what the hell?"

A thumping and continued screaming as Joey hurtled downstairs holding one arm, the skeleton on his sweater staining with blood. I caught him. At the top of the stairs loomed Adam Corlett, grasping the missing knife.

"He *moved*!" Adam's exaggerated eyebrows said, *This is far from my fault…*

The front door opened and Eleanor and her brother came back inside. Leon looked up carefully at Adam Corliss and said, "Ramo Samee?"

Adam nodded.

"The famous Indian knife-thrower?"

"Best in the world."

"… He missed."

"I *told* Joey not to move." Adam's was the plaintive voice of one who has always been misunderstood.

Darlene extracted her red phone and with red nails clicked 911. "What street number are we?"

"4137." I pulled the blood-soaked wool away from Joey's skin—his blood staining the white bones on his sweater skeleton. I looked down the neck-hole. Blood seeped but did not gush from his shoulder.

"You've got to be fucking kidding me," said Darlene into her phone. She snapped it shut.

"Is the ambulance coming?" I asked her.

"They said to take him there ourselves."

"What?"

"They asked was he breathing. They asked if he was conscious. If he's breathing and conscious they said we have to take him ourselves unless we want to wait an hour and fifteen minutes. Jesus H. Christ what are they driving, tricycles?"

"My Mazda's at Tyrone's Autobody," I said, "having a new timing belt put in."

"I'll call Casino Taxi," Darlene started dialing.

"No." Eleanor stepped into the midst. She stared at Adam as she told her brother, "Leon, go get Ed. Tell him to bring the car. Tell him Joey's hurt and he has to get here right away. Tell him his ghost did it." Adam stared back at her with an expectant expression that stopped just short of being a smirk. Leon went out and Eleanor got ice, lay Joey on the couch with his shoulder higher than his heart, and applied pressure. She made me give her a wooden spoon and the belt off my dress.

"What do you mean," I asked her, "his *ghost*?"

She manipulated the spoon against Joey's shoulder and tightened my belt around it. It was a pale blue, plastic belt, a half-inch wide, and had never been anything but decorative until now.

"Ed's ghost," she nodded toward Adam Corlett, "is what I call that kid. Always outside our house, doing circus tricks. Time and time again I used to call out to Ed and say, hey, look at the kid juggling, or on his stilts, or tossing balls around like a seal. Ed never came to the window. Then, one time, he finally came and looked, but he said he couldn't see the kid. He was right there, and Ed said he couldn't see anyone." Adam had slid halfway down the staircase, his back to the wall, and now watched Eleanor, subdued, waiting.

"Is that," he nodded at her improvised contraption with the belt and spoon, "a tourniquet?" He appeared only slightly interested, as if he'd heard of tourniquets but had not seen one made. Nothing in him suggested he felt responsible for or even slightly connected to the appearance of this example. The door burst open and Ed Dickson, furious, took in the scene on the couch then searched and fixed his sight on Adam, who at the moment Ed saw him abruptly flushed with vitality, his face pink with a white streak as his own blood infused his face and he shouted at Ed, indignant and familiar, "Don't blame *me*—I didn't do it on purpose!"

Ed Dickson had invisible restraints binding his arms and legs, which strained against an impulse to which the room

itself, its walls and light fixtures and the mantel piece looking on with disguised calm, knew he must not give in. Adam
flattened himself against the wall, its cold plaster his witness
and support. The other walls shrank imperceptibly, distancing
themselves—there was a surplus of stillness in the room. But
emotion had escaped both father and secret son: they had not
ceased glaring at each other. Ed Dickson didn't know where
else to look, and Adam stared at the one thing he wanted to
see above all others—his father's face, full of feeling directed
completely at him, Adam.

"Ed?" Eleanor said to her husband.

Adam Corliss's chin crumpled. He began to cry. He hung
his head and ran and slammed it against his father's ribs and
he held onto Ed Dickson and sobbed. Ed looked down at the
boy's head against his golf shirt that had embroidered on it one
of those little animals—a fox or a crocodile—I forget which
creature, and he did not embrace the boy. Eleanor kept her
eyes on her husband's face, but he would not look at her. I
tried to see Ed and Adam through her eyes in that instant—
Adam tearful and butting his gold hair pitifully into Ed's shirt,
wetting it—and to understand what, if anything, Eleanor
must now know, but it was hard to discern.

"The ghost," Eleanor had called Adam. Had she said *Ed's*
ghost? Had she seen the way Ed Dickson had looked at Adam
when he stormed in—looked *through* Adam—with a fury that
comes only out of connection deeper than any knife wound?
If she had any dignity, would Eleanor Dickson not now gather
her forces and breathe deeply before arranging to have the
locks changed and her husband sent quietly to one of those
grey-furnitured basements in Bedford or Lower Sackville
where disgraced husbands go to live on Tony's Donairs until
they meet a new and unsuspecting woman?

But it was difficult to read.

"Ed?" said Eleanor again.

She was a woman who'd grown up with an unstable brother and, I remembered her hinting, an alcoholic father: a woman who knew the world was full of unpredictable forces underlying any matter at hand. Eleanor Dickson was an expert at reminding people of the correct order of proceedings in any catastrophe. She kept her hair composed in a bobbed helmet ready for battle, serviceable during parent-teacher meetings or collapsing circus tents. But under it, I watched fall apart the red and cream lumps of her face. I glimpsed furniture and other large pieces of equipment being shifted within the darkness of her watchful eyes—stagehands clad all in black moved silently in that darkness rearranging her set. To us they were nearly invisible, but Eleanor knew their footfalls, their names, and the exact position of each tread as they surreptitiously rearranged everything in there, everything.

His Brown Face Through the Flowers

They had strung lights along the seafront in different shapes: stars, moons, diamonds, and they had openly said it was to cheer the people up. Francine had come home from Canada to be near her father. Her father had been ready to die. Now he had died, the funeral was over, and Francine was faced with the smallness of England for two more weeks until the date on her plane ticket. This was in 1986, and Francine was fifty-two. Lydia, her childhood friend, and Katie from her teenage years, had begged her to stay at their houses. They had been her maid and matron of honour. But she was going to stay in her father's flat and clear it out for whoever moved in next. He would have wanted that. She had cleared out the cupboards, the closets and the drawers, and she had scrubbed the flat. She had given the curtains and the china away to people who had come to the tea she had given after the funeral. She had had no sisters or brothers. Her mother was dead. Francine was the only one left. So if Lydia's mother had seen the china cups at the funeral tea and said, "My, these cups are nice Francine. What are you going to do with them when you go?" why not give them to her? Lydia's mother had eyed the flat then. It was bigger than her own, and she wondered about being put on the waiting list for people who were eligible to live in it. The smallness of England, Francine had thought again, and it was the first time she had come back and not wished to stay forever.

After the funeral tea she had gone to the telephone box at the top of Mile-End Road to call the Houses Cleared numbers advertised in the *Gazette*. She called two. One said he would come now, and one said he would come in the morning.

The first one was a young Asian who wore nice clothes and smiled. He was good-looking. She showed him the furniture. It was shabby except for two pieces: a writing table and a chest of drawers.

"I will give you a hundred pounds."

"Well, I'll consider your offer. I'll compare it with the others and I'll let you know."

"You have others coming to see you?" He looked hurt. "Why? Do you not believe I am giving you a good price?"

"I want to compare prices, that's all. I'll let you know if yours is best. I have to do the best I can."

"I will tell you what I will do." Every word precise and meticulous. He gesticulated with an elegant brown hand. She caught a faint and lovely scent. "I will give you a hundred and ten and I will clear the house of everything." He floated his hand toward the shabby couch and the chairs with their knees shining through the upholstery, "and that way you will not have to pay the council twenty pounds." Her friends had said she might have to pay the twenty pounds. Still, she did not relent.

"I'll see what the other people say and then I'll call you back." He went away then, graciously.

The next morning a fat man with greasy curls came to the door. He wore a shirt whose top button remained undone. Curls of hair showed. He wore a gold necklace, and bracelets and rings. He was a local, a northerner. They had been having record-high temperatures and he was sweaty. She showed him around.

"I'll give you twenty for that," he pointed to the chest of drawers, "and fifty for that," the writing table, "six for them and two for that." It added up to a hundred and eight pounds. She thanked him and told him she would let him know. He went out as if he didn't care.

In the afternoon she went to her father's tiny garden to gather silver dollar plants. He had not planted anything—glaucoma had made him blind—but seeds had drifted from someone else's patch and taken root, as if the seeds knew that she, who had gardened ever since she married, were coming to visit them. She had discovered them before the funeral and had been picking and peeling them. Peeled, they were tall stems decorated with shimmering pearl-coloured circles, and she had filled the room with them and given a bunch to everyone who had come to the funeral tea. There were still more in the garden. She had gathered an armload and was ready to take them inside, when the elegant first man appeared.

"What did he give you?" He did not appear insistent somehow. He seemed to be doing something he had promised her he would do, and she liked him for it. Not like the fat one dividing everything into bits.

"It was very similar to yours."

"Did he say he would clear the house of everything?"

"No."

"Well I will do it. I will give you a hundred and ten pounds and I will clear the whole house and you will not have to pay the council."

"All right."

"Good." She felt he said this word to her, not to himself as the other one would have done. She told him to come tomorrow.

That evening she wandered around the rooms drinking a glass of brandy that she kept replenishing from the flask she had hidden in the bathroom. The flask was left over from the funeral tea. Everybody had wanted the whiskey. There was a package of cigarettes in her purse too. She had never smoked. But there was the strain and the loneliness of the flat, and Lydia's telling her, "I couldn't get along without my menthols. Only the odd one mind you." So she had bought a pack of menthols. But these in her purse now were not menthol. She had graduated almost immediately to the real thing. With the curtains gone and the light on, she held her cigarette below the sill so her sons and daughter could not see it from their own windows across the Atlantic. Lydia was right. Cigarettes were great company. But she had not expected them to burn away so fast. You had to keep lighting one after another. And these were the longest you could get. Benson and Hedges. She would throw the pack away as soon as she got to the airport.

She rolled up the good sleeping bag that covered her father's bed and put it under her own bags. There were a couple of pictures on the walls. She took these down and tucked them in the same place. She even took the nails out in case they attracted his attention. She could give these things to people she cared about.

When he came the next day he looked around. "My, you are organized." But that was all he said. He counted out the money, "One hundred and ten," and gave it to her. There was a huge skinhead with him. She had been wondering how he would move everything. They began. Francine stayed in the middle of the living room, sitting on a cracked stool peeling silver dollars. A pile of them lay unpeeled near her left foot, and a peeled pile glimmered near her right. She had loved her father.

She looked up when they had gone downstairs for about the sixth time. There was a little carved night table left, painted black, and behind the door a big vase of artificial flowers that must, she thought, have been put there by one of the home help workers in a futile attempt to brighten the room. The vase of flowers was something she had thought about saving, but because it was so unwieldy, and because she loved real flowers, she had left it alone. She wondered if he would try to take it. He came back alone, picked the little night table up and stood there.

"That is it then," his modulated tones reached inside her like music. "And now you have a nice trip back to Canada." He inclined his head toward her, gracious and polite, yet somehow reassuring. As he approached the door he scooped the vase of flowers in his free arm, and then he went out.

He was unconscious of her watching him through the doorway. He had to stop and turn around the banister at the top landing. His arm encircled the vase and she could see his brown face through the flowers. Then there was just the banister.

She went to Lydia's house the day after that, with the sleeping bag and the pictures. The small house was full of people; Lydia's husband, their eldest daughter and her little boy and husband, their youngest daughter, and Lydia's mother. The youngest daughter was fifteen but Francine thought she looked like a little girl because she was wearing white socks and a skirt and her knees were knobbly. Fifteen-year-olds in Canada didn't look like that. They had a tea for her. Salmon buns, sausage rolls, cheese scones and lettuce and tomato. Trifle and chocolate cake and lemon meringue pie. Hot tea and milk and sugar and chocolate biscuits. The husbands were out of work. Lydia was taking a course in computers and cookery, and so was her husband. Francine's other friend Katie had told her these courses were just a limp go by an impotent government at raising people's hopes and nobody was fooled. Katie was working for the Labour party now, and she had a candidate's photograph in her living room window. That was another thing that was different. Francine had not thought Katie would ever join any sort of group.

The tea was lovely but Francine felt as if everyone in the small house was trapped. She kept longing to draw a deep draught of fresh air. She had been wanting that ever since she had come home. Maybe it was the heat. She felt her friends were hanging on to everything she told them, as if they imagined she held a key they did not hold. And when she told them about the man who came to clear her father's house, they wanted to know whom she had found. She described him. She told them how nice he was, how she had liked him. None of them knew whom she could have called. Then one of the husbands figured it out. "Oh," he said, "she means the Paki from Dean's Road."

Everyone's curiosity was satisfied, and they went on talking as before the terrible price of everything, how bad unemployment was getting, the smallness of England, how many foreigners there were now. And still they looked at her with that trapped expression that had an edge of eagerness, as if they wished she would hurry up and somehow release them instead of just sitting there eating the sausage rolls. They talked as if there were nothing mysterious in Francine's enthusiasm about meeting the Paki from Dean's Road, and before she could tell them he was someone she would never forget, they seemed to have forgotten he had ever been mentioned.

Handsome Devil

I was looking for something *new* on the bulletin board just inside the door of the Duckworth Lunch; a kiln firing on the beach—did I want a handmade bodhran?—when a handsome devil came in from the avenue and looked me up and down. I had a new haircut and my yellow dress and he said, "I haven't seen you around before."

The Duckworth Lunch had been my haunt ever since it used to be on the other side of the road, and now a lot of new people came in. Maybe this guy was one of them. I'd sort of preferred the old place—it's normally the disadvantages of a place that attract me. There was more sunlight now, and we had a sparkling view of the harbour and the war memorial, around which the daffodils had bloomed. Years ago, when I lived in an apartment across the road, I used to nip a cenotaph daff now and then to brighten up my windowsill, but my friend Janice Quigley saw me do it and said I should feel ashamed for removing flowers that had been planted in memory of men who had sacrificed their lives in both wars. In fact Janice Quigley has never been the same toward me since, which is too bad, because her reprimand was one of those moments when you know someone is absolutely right and there has been something amiss in your world view until now, in fact you have been brought up all wrong, and you try to change your behaviour accordingly. When I stole those daffodils and lived in that apartment, a man used to sit under the memorial's bronze fisherman spying at me until I noticed him and put up some curtains. But this man now, this handsome devil, was nothing like that creep. He was not going to throw up in one of the public wastebaskets anytime soon.

"Where do you live?" he took out a notebook.

"Dog's Pond Extension."

"How far is that from St. John's?"

"It's a forty-five minute drive."

He assessed this.

"On a day like today," I added. Real estate ads called it a half hour commute, which might have been true if you were manning a Formula One racing hovercraft. I liked to be honest about the length of that drive when anyone asked. Forty-five minutes was more or less accurate now, but come mid-February...

"Do you mind giving me your address so I can drive out and visit you tomorrow?"

I must have been feeling sunny because I scrawled a map on one of his pages with X marking the spot. "There's a wall of aspens. You have to keep peeping through gaps until you see a black house with a red roof."

I don't usually go in for handsome devils and they never take a second look at me under normal circumstances. My stars must have been aligned and sparkling upon me. I felt a little tug that said he was too clean-cut, that he didn't have enough disadvantages, but I tried to ignore it. I went home and tidied up the kitchen and swept the place and even used a bit of Mister Clean. The next morning I showered and put on my blue and white dress and an apron, and started making bread. I decided to complement my snappy new haircut with some wholesome homesteading skills and greet the handsome devil as if I whipped up loaves of bread all the time, their tops glossy with melted butter.

I realized he hadn't said what time he would come, so I aimed the loaves to come out of the oven at 11:30, and somehow in my mind I decided that he would arrive between then and 2:30 in the afternoon, so I made a pot of delicious soup. The thing about soup is that you can make great, amazing, killer-garlic and herb and crouton and whatever soup without a recipe, using things you happen to have in the fridge, and if you have a bit of ancient parmesan to grate into it so much the better. But by 2:30 there was still no sign of the handsome devil, and I started to get a bit miffed. I remembered his little notebook. What a fool I had been! And why should I make loaves and soup for the likes of him, and who was he and where did he live, anyway? Who was asking whom to prove what to whom here? And why was I putting up with it? I didn't even know the handsome devil. What right did he have ... and so on, until, at 4:30, there came a friendly sounding rap at my door. I amaze myself sometimes with the speed at which I can travel from condemnation to forgiveness. I glanced in the mirror and was pleased to see I still looked flushed from all the baking in a pretty sort of way, and I decided to leave my apron on as a sign of casual industriousness.

But lo and behold who should it be at the door but Janice Quigley's ex-husband, large as life with a rum gut and a set of groomed whiskers, and not the handsome devil at all.

"You're home," he said, as if he came to visit me all the time, and I remembered that he had a horse named Kitty, about which Janice had expressed impatience, and that every Christmas he dressed up in a red suit and hitched Kitty up to an old-fashioned carriage and went visiting distant cousins and business associates or anyone who he knew had children, around the bay—he and Janice were child-less. I knew this but I didn't know much else about Maurice Quigley, except I remembered his work had something to do with town water supplies and pipelines and reservoirs, and he was away a lot. And it was this work that brought him here that day. He had, he said, to look at some joints in the Murre's Hill pipeline.

"And I remembered old Janice sayin' you lived up this way, and it was such a great old day out there now and I have to dry out some of my new ducks and I wondered if you'd like to come along and take a look at them while I have them all laid out. Perfect ducks, they are, if I do say so myself."

"Ducks?"

"In my truck. Come out and see them for yourself. Take off that apron and come out with me to the site. I've got a bit of lunch on the go. Perfect day for it, come on girl." I could tell he was looking at me appreciatively, and while he was not my type of man—he had perhaps far too many disadvantages even for this lover of imperfections—I thought, why not. Why the hell not. So I whipped my apron bow undone and put on my cashmere cardigan and an Isadora Duncan scarf and left my homestead to itself and got in Maurice Quigley's Dodge Ram.

"So these are your ducks."

"Yup. Gessoed ready for a lick of paint after we dry them out for an hour or two."

The ducks were carved out of wood and had been coated in white.

"They must have taken hours to carve."

"Well what am I gonna do now Janice has gone and left me on my own in the nighttimes?" We were driving down Comerford's Road to the main highway. He started singing. *The silence of a falling star lights up a purple sky...* I noticed he had a mickey of rum sitting in the door pocket. I did not want to be part of some drunken ex-husband's duck-painting fantasy. What was I doing in the truck? Had the handsome devil's standing me up affected me so greatly I would stoop to this? But Maurice Quigley said, "Have a look in that hamper. Thin as a rail. You're like that fairy story where the girl sticks a twig out of her cage so the old witch won't eat her up because she's so scrawny. You need a bit of fat on your bones. Have a look."

I looked in the Coleman cooler that sat between us. We were going up Clarence Cove Mountain Road where the pipeline snaked down, a gravel road nobody went up except maintenance crews and teenagers. He swerved into a tiny clearing beside a one-window shack that had a chicken wire fence and a padlocked gate just as I laid my hand on a real French baguette, not the supermarket kind, and I saw a hunk of St. André cheese in there as well before he said, "Get the knife out, girl—cut yourself a piece before you waste away to nothing. Here." He pulled a Husky utility knife out of his pocket, sliced a sliver of the cheese and gave it to me. St. André cheese has a wallop of gorgeous butterfat flavour suffused with the merest hint of bacterial culture. I had been eating convenience store mild orange cheddar and Maurice Quigley might as well have injected me with some bliss-inducing drug.

"Come on," he said, "We'll get out and walk up the line and I'll set these ducks down to dry and I'll pour us a glass of wine and you can babysit my ducks while I go get to the bottom of the missing rivets at checkpoint seventeen." He collected the ducks in his arms like babies and gave me three to carry up the hill. He had a blanket rolled up under one arm and he laid it on some grass and showed me where he wanted the ducks laid out on the pipe in full sun, then he went back and got the hamper and a couple of wineglasses and poured some Bin 444 and we raised a glass there among the vetch and the hay and the pipeline that smelled faintly of tar.

"To ducks," he said, and cut me a piece of salami that was hard and transparent and had cracked peppercorn in it. The handsome devil who had not shown up could go straight to bloody hell. I thought about sex with the handsome devil, and with this pipeline maintenance duck painter whom Janice Quigley had, at one time, married. What was marriage, really, but an extension of the present moment, in which a woman might think, this is okay, sitting here by a pipeline in the sun. Better than some other marital situations. But of course Maurice Quigley and I were not married, and something in me could not be certain that either he or the handsome devil had sex in mind, concerning me. This was a blind spot I had. Somehow, despite years and even a lifetime of evidence to the contrary, a part of me persisted in thinking maybe these few men who expressed a slight interest in my company wanted human company that might not necessarily be sexual. They might want somebody to talk to and laugh with about the absurdities of the world. Everything did not necessarily lead, in their minds, to us taking off our clothes and having sex. I kept thinking this might be possible, and I know it seems foolish, but I sort of wished it were. I wished I could sit at the pipeline with Maurice Quigley and have great bread and cheese and wine and salami and a rip-roaring great discussion of life, without having to decide whether or not I was going to let him kiss me and take off my clothes and do things of which Janice Quigley would, again, perhaps even more than the military daffodils, take a dim view, and to which I myself took a less than enthusiastic shine.

"Janice never mentioned you make ducks," I decided to invoke both the ducks and Janice, thinking one or the other or perhaps both subjects might lift his own mind from any thoughts of rolling around on the embankment with me, in case it had gone in that direction.

"Janice never minded nothin' about those ducks," he said. "She didn't want to hear nothing about them. No." He was eating the salami delicately for a man of his type, I thought, and he reminded me of Bumper, a dog my old boyfriend once had, who took Vienna sausages into his mouth with a quivering finesse that was surprising, as if Bumper had been a human trapped in a dog's body, a thing that often occurs to me when I look at dogs. Maybe Maurice Quigley had been a bit more like the handsome devil in another life, and maybe the handsome devil was devolving into a next life in which his own appearance would match his abysmal manners. It was too bad, I thought, that the Maurice Quigleys of the world could be so underestimated based on their appearance. But by this time I was on my third glass of wine.

"But you," he said, "you know what you should make?"

"What?"

"Jellyfish."

I remembered a souvenir café off the wharf near Caplin Cove where a hermit woman made carrot cake and mermaid Christmas tree ornaments and thrummed trigger mittens and sold them to tourists from June to September. She hadn't made any jellyfish but her whole stretch of shoreline had been full of them and I had hung over her wharf licking cream cheese icing and looking at their lit-up trails and thinking how beautiful they were.

"What would you make jellyfish out of?" I asked Maurice Quigley.

"You, now. You could think of something. You could sell those jellyfish for three hundred dollars each."

"Is that how much people pay for your ducks?"

"People will pay," he said, "a lot more than three hundred dollars for a Maurice Quigley original."

"Really?"

"The last one I sold of this King Eider here," he pointed to a duck with a head that looked as if it wore a misshapen crash helmet, "a man down in Florida paid seven hundred and ninety five dollars for. You can have a look when I get it done, and you'll see. It's the carving and the detail. You gotta have really precision-made detailing and you can't let it go under the price that it's worth. Sometimes you have to wait. Jellyfish, now, you could make a killing if you went about it the right way. No one is making jellyfish, but you could."

"But isn't there, like, a duck market, hunters and the like? There are no jellyfish collectors, I don't think."

"You'd be surprised."

He went and checked the pipeline, then came back and wrapped up the remains of the salami and baguette—he was fastidious about not leaving any garbage on the landscape— and I thought he was about to roll up the blanket and descend back to his truck, when he said, pointing to his smallest white duck, "That one there now, is a real duck, just pretending to be made out of wood." He sat watching it, as if expecting its live properties to become manifest if we could only be still enough: a feather blowing off in the wind, an infinitesimal lift of wings. I sat motionless and joined in the game, and part of me was ready to believe him—the same part, perhaps, that had been equally willing to be swept off her feet by that handsome devil in the Duckworth Lunch.

"Have you ridden it?" I ventured. Not only was it alive, the smallest duck could also change in size, I surmised, and become a giant, fairytale duck, able—like a magic carpet— to transport us over this golden-grassed landscape and over the sea to who knew what sorts of minarets and gilded roofs.

I remembered reading that the crows of St. Petersburg had a habit of sliding down the golden shingles, purely for the joy of it, and that Russian officials were trying to exterminate them because the gold was real, and the crows were gradually wearing right through it, scattering gold dust in the air and rendering the shingles worthless and ordinary, like shingles in less glorious cities.

"You mean, have I gotten on its back and gone places?" He looked at me incredulously.

"Yeah." I challenged him with one of my serious expressions. The sun would soon go down. This land had golden hollows in it. We were not exactly drunk, and he was not exactly ugly, not any more. I found his idea about making jellyfish beautiful; his ducks unfinished and full of promise. The handsome devils of the world knew nothing about certain enchantments. They had a sense of entitlement. They went around getting women to jot their addresses in little notebooks, and they visited or did not visit these women whenever they felt like it. Whereas this man…

"I have not spoken to a soul about my travels on that there duck," he said. He looked at me carefully. I had the feeling he was really and truly assessing whether or not I could be trusted with the precious jewels of his innermost journeys through duck heaven.

I had gone too far. There were too many things about Maurice Quigley that I found coarse and uninviting. I wished I had kept my mouth shut about flying on his smallest duck. But it was too late. I knew it was too late. Some men, those with the most heaped and various collections of disadvantages, have no way of going back home once someone has peeped inside and found their hidden beauty. They can't help themselves—they are in love with you for life. You will find them knocking at your door, three, four, five, even ten years from now, at four in the morning if need be, unable to give up on that one brief glimpse with which you, heartless and fresh from your own comedown in the world, tantalized them with an intimation of hopeless love. Sometimes it becomes necessary to telephone the police.

Darlings' Kingdom

WE HAD OUR GYPSY CARAVAN up for rent and the calls coming in were not good. I felt like apologizing to our birch trees, and our magic fire pit, and to the partridges who had nested faithfully near us all the while we'd lived in the glade.

"Is there room for me to bring my own couch?" asked the first caller. "I'm afraid one of my cats… I mean the urine is pretty much cleaned, but…"

Or—"Hold it for me. Do not move on this issue. I am coming up from Montana right now—my girlfriend has—I'm gonna be suicidal if—promise me you won't rent this place to anyone before I get there. It's divinely ordained for me."

That second caller arrived in a coat bearing extravagant fringes and an embroidered pueblo. His license plate was not from Montana and he strode around led by his solid beer gut and unable to see anything from under that hat, then disappeared forever.

"I'm getting desperate," I told Frank, who had painted the baseboards and installed a double valve on the gas tank for the stove. "I'm almost ready to consider renting it to Gus Darling after all."

"I thought you weren't quite sure about Gus. You said if he was anything like his father…"

"Sons usually are either like their fathers or as unlike them as humanly possible."

I had met Gus after my friend Norma started giving him blowjobs on the highway down to his family's farm in Pencil Cove. Gus was a Darling, and the Darlings had driven anyone who was not a Darling out of Pencil Cove a generation before, and now they were starting on each other. They had a spring lamb operation down there, and they made cranberry juice that they exported all over the northeast under their own label and also under labels they had sold to a few supermarket chains. The cranberries grew all over Pencil Cove and it was a beautiful sight to see them shining like rubies, or when they were in flower the place was covered in a snowy bloom whose perfume mingled with the sweet stench of briny bladderwrack mixed with rotted fish, stinking yet lovely enough to ignite all the forlorn longing of the heart. I loved to breathe the salty shock, fishy and weedy yet horribly lovely. The smell of Darling territory was both horror and exhilaration and it reminded me I was part of the world's wild and ongoing death.

To get there you had to drive down a shore guarded by ancient junipers the wind had tortured into petrified gyrations, and my friend Norma had loved being one of the only people on earth allowed to go there, because most people found themselves in the sights of Gus's or his father's rifle as soon as they came over the hill that led to that beautiful, self-contained valley.

"Gus's not bad," Frank said. "He's just sick of his old man having him on a short leash. He said to tell you if you'd agree to rent our place to him to give you this now," Frank handed me nine hundred dollars in a Pencil Cove Cranberries envelope, "and he'll move in the day we leave to make sure Roddy Holloway doesn't burn the place down, and if ever the roof leaks or the pipes break while we're away he'll fix everything."

"Cash—so … he means it?"

"Gus likes our place. He likes how it's hidden in the trees. And it's a bit closer to his ex-girlfriend and his little girl in town. He loves going to see his little girl."

"Maybe we should invite him to our going away party."

So we invited Gus and he drove up with a pickup load of fresh crab and a twenty-gallon pot. He stationed himself at our sink rinsing and cracking legs and tossing crab in boiling water and draining mountains of it and giving it to our guests like some sort of hired seafood chef from the new boutique hotel in Baird's Cove.

Our guests were Grampa Bob who likes to give teenagers wine and get them dancing around our birch trees to piss off their parents, and Gordon Hullimer who is serious about his black belt and who had his toilet put in on a diagonal so he wouldn't bump his head, and Gordon's wife Calista who owns a small bookstore and who lost her leg when she was a teenager and looks for the good in everyone. My friend Norma had been banned by the Darling family from giving Gus any more blowjobs or from entering Pencil Cove ever again, but she came with lipstick on her teeth, half an hour before the arrival of her ex-husband Trevor, who tended to get on his high horse and who was not speaking to Norma either now that he had a Korean wife. I did not feel like speaking to Norma myself, since she had on a previous visit ruined my best blanket by wrapping my goat in it. I had not invited Norma but she had found out about the party and she was your quintessential gatecrasher.

With all this going on we did not notice for some time how much beer Gus drank as he flung his endless supply of fresh crab onto the picnic table Frank had nailed together out of two sawhorses and a barn door. We noticed it only when he started insulting people in a most literate way that seemed more eloquent than his usual way of speaking, which was somewhat shy and restrained, although always laced with a kind of wildness that I had supposed came from living in Pencil Cove with the cranberries and the cattle and his father who had a sideline outside cranberry season mapping growth patterns of shoreline plants for the federal government using a set of extremely precise instruments that he kept in a turquoise box of which he seemed very proud, since he did not have a degree—in fact Gus's father had not finished high school—yet the government trusted him more, it appeared, than it trusted any silken-arsed biologist from the university. Gus was saying this to Trevor, an example of a silken-arsed biologist if ever there was one, as I crossed the room to get more limes for the Corona.

When Trevor gets offended he does so in the traditional English way—I mean he quietly swallows his outrage like thumbtacks or staples which proceed to agonize and knot his innards so that just before he leaves the party in a silent rage he is forced to strut around making jerky movements like a marionette with a nervous tic, but he will never say anything impolite, except to stutter an occasional, "Now—look here!" Gus Darling loves that. He doesn't understand it but he loves to see it and he will do anything to make it last longer, including telling Trevor his ex-wife gives half decent blow jobs but it's no bargain because first you have to get her loaded and then you can't get rid of her, not like your new wife there, hey, buddy? She looks like a more sensible young woman altogether. In fact, Gus said, Trevor's new wife had just told Gus that yes, she'd like to come down to Pencil Cove herself to help him and his father with the cranberries. You needed a certain type of woman for cranberries. Women, Gus said, were cranberryish or they were not.

Gus started next on black belt Gordon's wife Calista, asking her what was it like anyway, to go around on one leg—that was something he'd often wondered and now here she was in front of him, a woman with only one leg, so he might as well ask her, she didn't mind, did she? "It's not every day you get to ask a one-legged woman how it feels."

The thing is, you can ask Calista Hullimer that kind of question and she won't take any offense—she'll just assume you're asking out of basic human decency and a wish to understand your fellow man or woman, and she'll even find it refreshing after going through a life in which nearly everyone pretends not to notice a thing about her physique. Plus Gus is a handsome guy—he's one of those blonde fellows with wickedness gleaming out of green eyes and he can get away with anything if you haven't known him very long. But I was starting to get to know him a bit better here at our party. I was starting to think he'd better watch out or Gordon Hullimer might show us all the thing I had secretly been wondering, which was how could a man so miniature yet so self-inflated have become a black belt in karate. I believe the reason he had insisted on having his toilet installed on a diagonal was that it was under the stairs. It was next to his den, and a taller man would, had the toilet been installed squarely against the wall, have had to crouch in order to pee. Gordon Hullimer could have stood straight, but he wanted a normal man's headroom. I don't know what he said to Gus Darling, I just know Gus stopped his assembly line of crab legs, the most delicious any of us had known, and he came out and hunkered in the deepening dusk to which some of us had escaped, and showed Grampa Dob's three-year-old grandson what transpired if you threw a Bic lighter into the heart of marshmallow coals. I was pretty sure this was the kind of thing they did for fun in Pencil Cove when Gus Darling was a little boy, and I know there used to be road signs along that part of the shore warning people not to use deep fat fryers.

"So Frank gave you my nine hundred dollars?" Gus Darling let the length of his thigh lean on mine and his thigh was warm and I have to admit I liked it.

"He did."

"You won't be sorry you rented your house to me. First off, I'm gonna go in those woods and you know what I'm gonna do?"

"No."

"What's wrong with those fellows who live in that house beyond the marsh? They call it a seniors' home but that's no seniors' home, is it, now. What do they call it? The Heavenly Home for Nitwits?"

"Rest Haven. It's a home for men who can't look after themselves. One of them might come over: Nathan. He usually comes over and has a beer when we have the fire lit and people over." I liked Nathan. When he first came to live at Rest Haven I called the night shift worker and asked if he had a psychotic criminal history because he stalked the woods looking like a cross between John the Baptist and Rasputin, but I grew to like him. "Nathan's all right. He's a bit clairvoyant."

"Well when I'm living here The Amazing Nathan won't be coming over for any more beers if he knows what's good for him." Gus took a swig and gave me an intimate stare. "You never asked me what the first thing is that I'm gonna do once you and your man are gone and I'm here with full run of this place."

"What might that be?"

"I'm gonna check out the boundary markers and move them, bit by teensy little bit, so the people who own the heavenly home for nitwits and the other people on the other side will have their land shrink every day. They won't know it, but I'm gonna put down stakes and razor wire and gradually make this piece of territory into a fine little kingdom. Then I'll get my old

Winchester out and if one of those retarded fellows even thinks about coming over onto my property I'll…" he pantomimed shooting Nathan's brains out and I wished I had not taken his nine hundred dollars, but what was I to do? We were leaving in less than a week. I loved the men at Rest Haven. Twice since we had lived here, one or another of them had gone missing in the marsh or in the woods and the police had come with their dogs, and the men had survived on pond water and berries and we had all worried about them a great deal, because aside from Nathan, who had a spectacular intelligence, they were all meek and a little lost. I couldn't stand the idea of them tripping over Gus Darling's razor wire or encountering him in the state to which he was progressing, which I now saw to be what they call a nasty drunk, and which I had not entirely expected, since I had never seen his father drink a drop.

It was the house I loved. I really did look at it as a gypsy caravan. There were blue-bead lilies and Linnaea Borealis under the trees, and every night we heard the steep brook, and we heard snipe in spring and toads in July and there was the mountain topped with a dusting of snow and stars glittering, truly glittering like stars in my Hilda Boswell nursery rhyme book, and the going away party should have been for the house, not for the people—but Frank was the people-lover in our little family, not me. What was wrong with me? The only person in our neighbourhood that I would be really sorry to leave was Rasputin, and he was crazy. Everyone else was so misshapen and self-absorbed I could not love them. I was not a person who could love people in their brokenness, like someone out of a *Guideposts* magazine, of which I'd had a steady diet growing up, as there were always back-issues in the magazine rack next to the toilet of the woman for whom I babysat the most. I did not love Grampa Bob, nor Gordon Hullimer, nor Trevor on his high horse. I sort of loved Norma, even when she'd accused me of failing to protect my goat from the north wind, but it was impossible to carry on a conversation with her since she persisted in sociopathic monologues. One time I had realized I might love Gordon Hullimer's wife Calista but only when she was alone with me, at which point she stopped looking for the good in everyone and became downright acerbic. If the truth were told, I supposed the person I most loved at our going away party was Gus Darling, the least lovable of them all, and the one from whom I most avidly wanted to distance myself now he had proven to be a maniacal alcoholic exploding gas lighters near the face of a sweet little three-year-old, getting him excited and possibly sowing seeds of a future arsonist.

"I'd drain that swamp," Gus said, pointing at our enchanted bog where snipe made their haunting calls that sounded like voices but were really the wind winnowing through their tail-feathers as they plunged from moon to marsh, and where a duck sheltered her young each spring from the crazed hunters in the town below, "and I'd set snares and live on local rabbits all winter. Between that and those ducks getting fat down beyond them alders, I'd be able to live off this property. You have no idea about squatters' rights do you, Violet Wainwright? Who in the name of God gave you a name like that? I never knew anyone with a name like that before who wasn't some ninety-year-old church woman with her mouth all scrunched like the asshole of my father's sow. Not that I'm saying that about your mouth, now Violet, don't go getting offended—I think I've offended your friend over there with the short legs, and his wife with only one leg, and that other one over there with the grandkid—I was only showing him how to make sparks. Jesus, you have a sensitive bunch of friends, Violet. They won't be coming around when I'm living here, I can guarantee you that … Squatters' rights."

Despite certain past adventures and odd accidents I was an innocent person in the ways of alcoholism and certain infidelities and a host of other normal human behaviour. I had read far too many *Guideposts* and they had so thoroughly skewed my view of human nature that I ended up loving all the wrong people, especially at parties. I couldn't tell a thing about a person's real character if we were at a party. Maybe nobody could. But the house. The house was talking to me. *Get Gus Darling out of here*, it said. *Give him back his nine hundred dollars. Tell him the deal is off.*

I did not want my house to be lonely. Grampa Bob's wife Rachel had arrived with homemade cheese puffs and was now visibly weeping on my husband's shoulder because she loved him in a way that she imagined I did not love him—Grampa Bob felt the same. I believe they wished they could keep Frank at their house because he is Herculean, and they were not happy that I was taking him away. Everyone at our going away party would miss Frank and Frank would miss them.

But the house, and the grey jays and the partridges roosting in the magical, huge silver birches at night, I would miss that, and it would miss me, though I am not lovable and apparently do not know how to love. I could not let the telephone caller with her urine-tainted couch rent my house, nor would I allow the compulsive liar in the world's best jacket, and no matter how much deep-seated and misplaced affection I had for Gus Darling, I could not let him set razor wire and rabbit snares all over the woods while he drank himself to oblivion and set the place ablaze and maybe even murdered or was murdered by Nathan depending on how clairvoyant Nathan might be on killing day. No. I had to put a stop to it, and I did. I went upstairs, took the nine hundred dollars from under the multi-head screwdriver in my underwear drawer, and placed it in Gus Darling's hand.

"I figured you were too much of a pussy to have me in your house," he said with a charming grin as he took the money somewhat eagerly. I realized he might have stolen it from the cranberry business, and that had I not invited Gus Darling to our going away party and found out what he was really like, had I sacrificed my gypsy caravan to his projected swath of destruction, it would have been the last cent I'd have seen from him. "Did I scare you?"

"You wanted to scare me." I was guessing but I continued. I do that a lot. When crazy people or bullies or manipulative people zero in I try to camouflage myself with guesswork. Sometimes I'm almost as clairvoyant as Nathan. "You'd like to try to scare me. Razor wire!" I laughed in Gus's face. "Squatter's rights!"

"Yes, Miss Violet Wainwright. Tell me that's not your real name. You look more like a Jenny Wren to me. Little Jenny Wren, like in one of them English poems. That's what I'm gonna call you. Tell you what. I'll take the money back but I'll hold onto it for you until you change your mind. It's yours. You won't rent this place to anyone else. Not in a hundred years. Not in a million years. No one wants a place built out of old two-by-fours and painted that colour and stuck hidden here in the woods away from everyone except that place full of lunatics beyond those trees. You're like Snow White and the Seven Dwarfs up here. Only another Snow White would want to move here, and only if she had some very strong dwarves to help her with the firewood and the well and the chimney and all the things you have your big husband do for you—he's big and strong but he's not exactly interesting is he, Jenny Wren?"

"He's interesting enough."

"Is he now?" Gus took a swig of his beer. "Yeah, I bet he's a real thrill. I bet he keeps you up at night talking about

Wilton-forged super junior C-clamps and chimney flashing and gutters for your screen porch." He looked at her and she looked back at him and they both knew this was true.

"No," Gus carried on, "there aren't that many Snow Whites around any more. But there's one dwarf. There he is in the yard right now, married to that one-legged woman. But he's no good to you. You need me to look after this place, and I'm going to do that for you. You don't need to worry about a thing. I'll look in on it, and I won't let that delinquent Roddy Holloway come in here and piss all over the walls or steal the furniture, and I'll even plant a few cranberries down by the marsh. You should see how well cranberries would do in a place like this. You should have started a second career here yourself, growing a few cranberries. I'll do that for you. This house won't be lonely at all, Jenny Wren. Not with me around."

"I don't think so, Gus. I think your number is up..."

Gordon Hullimer approached us. I had always imagined his particular black belt might have been like having a diploma from one of those correspondence schools that ask you to copy a line drawing of a dog in the back of a comic and mail it in as your entrance exam.

"He looks like a young radish about to explode," said Gus. "You know them peppery little radishes? That's about as much hurt as he could inflict on anyone. A speck of pepper in your eye. Harmless. Irritating though."

"I've called you a taxi, Mr. Darling. You'll be out of here, please, as soon as that taxi gets here."

"I'm all right, kind sir."

"You're not all right. You're drunk and you've insulted everyone at the party. I for one am so angry that I'm willing to pay the taxi driver myself to get you out of here."

"No worries, I was just about to leave. I've got my truck."

"You're a menace. A truck? You're so drunk you'd wrap your truck around the first pedestrian you saw."

"Pedestrian?"

"A Shore taxi will be here in fifteen minutes." Gordon Hullimer walked away. I knew we were a fifty-dollar cab ride from anywhere Gus Darling wanted to go.

Gus carefully placed his bottle upright in the grass and stood up.

"You're not getting in your truck."

"I've only got one problem."

"You're so drunk you can hardly stand?"

"I can stand just fine. And I can get home just fine. But I need you to do something for me, Jenny Wren. I need you to come down to my truck for a second."

My problem is that even when I know things are really bad, and I should take a stand, I often do not take a stand. There is something gullible about me, something dangerously passive and stupid.

"Why do you need me to come down to the truck?"

"Don't worry. I won't eat you. It'll only take a second."

"You can't drive like that."

"No, no, no, you don't know what I'm talking about. Just come."

"Wait for the taxi."

"The taxi, yeah. I'll wait for the taxi. I promise. Come on. Come down to the truck and help me out for just a second. Get away from these losers and ne-er-do-wells and people who have no curiosity about anything. If a big purple moon rose over that mountain next to the ordinary gold moon, none of them would even notice. Hell if the purple moon ate the other moon and then ate them they'd keep talking to each other about the price of tables at Ikea. Come on. I've got something I want to show you."

His truck was green but it did not have chrome like his father's truck. Gus's truck was comparatively modest. He opened the driver's door and sat at the wheel, which made me feel very jittery. I did not want Gus Darling driving down over our road in that truck in his condition.

"I want you," he said, "to sit in my lap for a second."

I did feel a frisson about Gus Darling, about all the Darlings for that matter, but even I knew it was not a frisson a person should heed, nor act upon in even the smallest way. I had, if truth be told, been in Gus Darling's father's truck a couple of times, and Finian Darling had called me long distance to tell me I meant the world to him, but that was before I was with Frank, with whom I was going away in less than a week to our new life far from here.

"No."

"Come on, girl, do me this one last little favour."

Some drunken scoundrels' laps are irresistible, that's all I can say. Gus's father had once told me his ancestors' bones floated underwater out beyond the Seal Rocks in Pencil Cove. The bones glowed in the weeds; they waltzed with flounder and cod that glittered like topaz and rubies. No Darling minded dying after the kind of life only a Darling knew how to live. No suburban graveyard for a Darling, and no tame, domesticated life either. Finian Darling said the word domesticated with a snarl. Both father and son strode around in brown and green fabric as if they'd donned the moss and earth that covered Pencil Cove, and they smelled like the ground of that place, the scent in cranberry blossom. I never saw either of them wear a primary colour. They wore only what Robin Hood might have worn, and I knew for a fact some of it was hand-stitched because I'd done a bit of mending on Finian Darling's leather sleeves, which might seem a bit servile but I know I am not the first to succumb to these romances of the

Darlings. Gus had a woman, Stacey, who stayed with him long enough to have a little daughter. It turned out, Gus told me now, that Stacey had in place a court order stating that for him to see his little girl, Millie, he had to have this contraption put in his truck.

"You breathe into it, here, see, and it measures your blood alcohol, and if it falls under the limit you can work the ignition for me. You've only had one or two drinks, haven't you? Millie does it for me all the time and she's only three. She sits in my lap and blows into this thing and off we go, me and my little girl. I don't drive with Millie when I've had as many drinks as I've had with you today, mind. This is an exception. Come on. Make a little puff in here for me and we'll get out of here together. I'll take you down to Pencil Cove and I'll show you my grandmother's secret bakeapple patch. Cranberries are one thing, but bakeapples... you've never lived until you've tasted bakeapples from Pencil Cove."

I did not tell Gus Darling that I'd already tasted bakeapples from Pencil Cove, that I'd lain down in the bakeapple bushes with his father, or that I also knew the whereabouts of his grandmother's secret blackberry patch, and her chanterelle patch, and the rose petal sachet in her cotton sheets whose scent I had breathed in the arms of his father while Gus's grandmother was out picking blackcurrants, which were my real favourite, and which grew in abundance on Pencil Cove's southwest banks. I might not know how to love people like Gordon Hullimer or Grampa Bob or Rachel or Norma or Trevor on his high horse, but I know how to love a place. I know how to listen to the voice of a brook and I know how to eat the kind of eels whose flesh in Pencil Cove is white and sweet when eaten with toast burnt over a clandestine beach fire. I know all these things, and I knew them as I sat in Gus Darling's lap in his old green truck, and I longed for that sweet white eel flesh and the blackcurrant musk and the high voltage connection with a Darling even if it was the son and not the father, and part of me did something terrible. Part of me breathed into that machine, the part that is seduced by places but not people, at least that's what I tell myself now, and off we careered down our hill. I remember that even as we began down the hill and I thought about how drunk Gus was and how this was an impossible, criminal thing I was doing, a thing that could never be forgiven, I imagined it would be easy to open the door and jump out before he ventured onto the main highway. I could open that door onto our little road, the safe road, the road back to my own life, and I could leap out easily. Our dog had done it once on the Witless Bay Line, and I had jumped out of a Volkswagen near Stephenville the time I'd realized my fishing companion, who was perhaps senile, had sparks showering from her tailpipe as we approached a biker-gang's encampment on the Hansen highway.

So I knew leaping was an option.

If I felt like leaping.

ACKNOWLEDGMENTS

THANK YOU TO MY EDITOR, John Metcalf, for your unparalleled insight, intuition and expertise, and for the valuable time and support you have dedicated to myself and to other authors whose work you have helped bring forth. Thank you to Daniel Wells at Biblioasis for your editorial advice, kindness and diplomacy. Thank you to my agent, Shaun Bradley, for your clear vision, good sense, and strong advocacy. Thank you to my family and friends for your companionship and love. And thank you, dear reader.

I thank the editors of the following publications in which earlier versions of some of these stories appeared:

The Walrus: *Madame Poirer's Dog*

Rattling Books audio anthology Earlit Shorts: *His Brown Face Through the Flowers*

CBC's Brief Encounters series: *The Zamboni Mechanic's Blood*

The Pottersfield Portfolio: *A Plume of White Smoke*

CNQ: Canadian Notes and Queries: *You Seem a Little Bit Sad*

JESSICA AUER

KATHLEEN WINTER's debut novel, *Annabel*, was nominated for the Orange Prize, the IMPAC Dublin Award, the Giller Prize, the Governor General's Award and The Writers' Trust Award; it won the Thomas Head Raddall Award (2011) and an Independent Literary Award (2010); it was selected as a *New York Times* Editor's Choice for 2011, became a #1 Canadian bestseller, and has been translated around the world. Winter's first story collection (*boYs*, Biblioasis, 2007) also won numerous Canadian awards. Born in the UK, Winter now lives in Montreal after spending many years in Newfoundland.